Performance Enhancing Drugs and Adulterants: The Hidden Assassin II

Alan H.B. Wu, Ph.D.

Performance Enhancing Drugs and Adulterants: The Hidden Assassin II contains fictitious characters, events, and places. Any resemblance to actual persons, living or dead, business establishments, events, or locales is entirely coincidental. The science described in these stories, however, is factual.

ISBN-13: 978-09973686-7-3
eBook ISBN: 978-0-9863634-1-2

Dedication

This book is dedicated to my wife who continues to challenge me to bring out the best in me. I acknowledge Patricia Beatty of the Palo Alto Medical Foundation and Stephanie Chan of the Hematology Laboratory at San Francisco General Hospital for their review of the manuscript.

Table of Contents

Prologue

In my first book, *Toxicology! Because What You Don't Know Can Kill You,* I wrote a story called "Urine Luck." It is about Jaco who abuses drugs, and Calvin a man whose responsibility is to do drug testing in my laboratory. Jaco is a bus driver and has to undergo regular urine drug testing to keep his job. Because Jaco is unable to get off drugs, he learns about adulterants; chemicals that he can add to his urine to invalidate test results. Calvin notices that one of the anonymous urine samples he tests regularly is unusual and suspects that the donor has been cheating with adulterants. But he has to follow lab policies for drug testing and we are unable to report his suspicion. Tragedy strikes Calvin's family as a result. With his knowledge of adulteration and drug testing, Calvin leaves my lab and turns his attention to the dark side. His influence on what happens to others becomes vast. Calvin hooks up with a former con artist to form a company manufacturing adulterants and masking agents. Given the large number of individuals who are tested for drugs of abuse, his legal business flourishes. Soon, he branches off into making hormones and drugs designed to improve performance. These compounds are used by athletes in order to gain a competitive advantage.

This book describes how Performance Enhancing Drugs work and how they can adversely affect the lives of athletes and the people around them. There are other stories of maladies affecting other well-known athletes and important individuals in history. However, the characters in these stories are fictitious.

Urine Luck

In high school there are the preppies, the jocks, the drama queens, the nerds, and the potheads. Jaco Jamison was clearly in the last category. He spent much time in the bathroom smoking cigarettes or an occasional joint before attending class. "I'm never going to need to know this shit," he told his mother. His mother knew that he wasn't dumb, just unmotivated. His car reeked of cigarette and marijuana smoke. Butts and crumpled rolling papers crammed the dashboard ashtray. He kept his windows closed for fear that the smell would reveal him to the school narcs, but everyone knew what he was up to anyway and didn't care.

Jaco was always good with cars and motorcycles. The kids brought all their mechanical problems to him. So when Jaco left high school, his classmates were not surprised that he was able to land a steady job as a garage man at the city's bus depot. By then, he was smoking dope regularly, yet it didn't interfere with his job. He became a master at concealing his drug use from his superiors. He worked at the bus depot garage for eight years and they eventually transferred him to driving the city's bus. This was easier than working on engines. The promotion, however, required him as well as other drivers, to undergo routine urine drug and alcohol testing.

Jaco did not want to lose his new job by failing a urine

test; he needed the money to support his drug lifestyle. He was able to stop smoking hash for a month while he started his new job. In the meantime, he learned all he could about drug testing policies and procedures so he could beat them. If he had studied this much in high school, he could have been a lawyer by now. One of the first things he found out was that you can buy at-home urine drug testing kits on the Internet. These tests were similar to the lab based test his employer used. Although purchasing these kits on a regular basis got expensive, it was better than losing his job with a positive drug test. The bus company always scheduled their drug test quarterly. Since they did not do them randomly, Jaco's plan was to abstain from smoking five days prior to the appointment. He tested his own urine using the kit just to be sure.

"If I test positive, I'll just call in sick that day," he told his unemployed co-druggie roommate. This plan worked for several years. But he wanted more. He believed he could beat the system without even having to stop smoking before the test.

Why should I cease my enjoyment four times a year? he thought. His new plan was to drink copious amounts of water to dilute his urine just prior to self-testing. Jaco learned that in order for his urine to come out positive, the amount of drug in the urine had to exceed the test's threshold. He had this down to a science; he knew exactly how much he could smoke and how much water he needed to drink to get below the test cutoff. Besides, he always owned the 'I am sick today' excuse as his get out-of-jail card. This worked for years. He knew he was playing with fire, but he didn't want to get off pot.

*

Calvin was in the nerd set in high school. His parents

emigrated from Taiwan when he was two years old. He did well in math and made friends through the science club. He was small for his age having reached puberty later than the other boys. He was shy around girls at school; most of them were bigger than he was. While they went to the same school, Jaco and Calvin didn't know each other. Their only encounter was when Calvin was a freshman and Jaco was in his fifth year of high school. Calvin desperately had to pee before algebra. Not knowing the unofficial bathroom rules, he went into the smoker's john. Jaco and his friends saw the little kid, pushed him against a stall, and told Calvin to beat it. After that encounter, Calvin said to himself, *someday I'm going to stand up to those guys.*

Calvin went to college, majoring in chemistry. Science was easy for him, and he was eager to learn. Right out of college, he got a job in my toxicology laboratory. We were doing workplace drug testing at the time. Calvin's job was to process the hundreds of urine samples each day and load them into the instruments for testing. He felt overqualified for this work, but he had to start somewhere. The worst part of the job was the awful smell. Sometimes, he would spill some urine onto his clothes, shoes, and socks. Fortunately we had a shower in the lab and he kept extra clothes on hand. I recognized that Calvin had a keen eye for details, and I wanted him to advance.

After a few years, I asked Calvin, "Why don't you go back to school and earn your master's degree in forensic science, which includes those involved with workplace drug testing? Then we can have you do more interesting jobs that suit your talents." With that encouragement, Calvin enrolled in night school while keeping his day job working for me. When Calvin finished two years later,

3

I promoted him to certifying scientist. His new job was to look at toxicology data and verify their results. By now, he was no longer the shy introverted person he'd been when he was young. Calvin met a girl, got married, and together they had a daughter named Jenny.

*

Jaco's urine sample was routinely sent to the lab for testing. Unknowingly, Calvin had been involved with Jaco's urine testing for years. The samples were identified by number only. Jaco's samples were simply labeled as #32449. In going through his daily records, Calvin noticed that one sample reported as negative was just below the cutoff for THC. THC is tetrahydrocannabinol, the active ingredient of marijuana. This sample also contained a low level of creatinine. While creatinine is a normal component of urine, low values indicate urine dilution by higher than normal fluid intake. Calvin went back into the records and found that #32449 consistently produced these results. He came to my office to show me what he had discovered.

I told him, "Some people have other drugs or constituents in their urine that may trigger a false reaction to the THC test. Our cutoffs differentiate between what is truly positive from interferrents. Besides, people can have small amounts of marijuana in their urine due to passive exposure. Calvin, you wouldn't want us to report a positive result just because someone was at a rock concert and exposed to others who were smoking, would you?"

"I guess not," he said. But Calvin wasn't satisfied. How could #32449 be at a rock concert each time he was drug tested? Although he knew he could get in trouble for this, Calvin kept one of #32449's urine samples aside in the freezer. He removed it one

4

day when I was away. Opening the cup, he let it stand at room temperature to let some of the water evaporate. When this concentrated urine was retested, it came out positive. *I've got my eye on you #32449*, he said to himself, and then discarded the cup.

Jaco's driving record was without incident. This eventually landed him a job driving kids at his old high school. They were mostly freshmen and sophomores who didn't have drivers' licenses yet or whose parents couldn't afford cars for them. He was ten years older than most of them and they treated him like he was Fonzie from Happy Days; the cool driver dude. He still had to undergo regular drug testing and he still was participant #32449. By this time, he'd gotten tired of drinking excess fluids prior to his tests and learned about adulteration products. He purchased Urine Luck from the Internet in hopes of taking his deception to the next level. Urine Luck was a commercially available urine drug-testing adulterant. It consisted of a vial containing one ounce of a yellow fluid. It arrived through the mail in an unmarked package. The user was instructed to add the liquid in the vial to a urine sample while in the privacy of the bathroom before submitting the specimen to the urine collector. Urine Luck oxidized drugs to other compounds, thereby producing a false negative urine drug test result. Jaco tried it out with his at-home drug testing kit and found that it worked for marijuana. By this time, he also began experimenting with heroin. Urine Luck worked on this drug too. Jaco went online and purchased enough of the adulterant to last him for three years of quarterly drug testing.

Back in the lab, Calvin noticed something was now different about #32449's urine. His previous urine samples were odorless and colorless, a reflection of his dilute urine. Now, this sample was not near the threshold value, and had a much deeper yellow color. The creatinine level was also now within normal limits. Calvin thought that maybe #32449 had reformed and was now clean. But then he thought, *I don't buy it. He's doing something else*. On a whim, and totally against the rules, Calvin took a solution of THC and added it to one of #32449's samples that previously tested negative. To his astonishment, the repeated test remained negative, even though the added THC should have produced a positive result.

He is definitely doing something again, Calvin thought. *In order to solve this problem, I have to think like a drug user trying to hide my addiction. What would I do if he were me?* Calvin knew that subjects who are drug tested urinate in the privacy of a bathroom without a witness. Maybe #32499 was adding some chemical to invalidate his test. So he went on Google and typed in "adulteration and urine drug testing." There was a hit for Urine Luck. After reading about how this adulterant worked, Calvin came straight to my office. "Do we have permission to test suspicious urine samples for the presence of adulterants such as this?" he asked, showing me the Internet article. I emphatically replied, "We can't do that today. Taking that sort of action would be viewed as a witch hunt. But I'm part of a group of toxicologists who are trying to get the regulations changed so that we *can* do this type of testing. For now, though, we have to be careful that we don't single anyone out." With that Calvin bit his tongue and went back to his office.

About two years later, fervor about adulteration practices did lead to changes in the federal drug testing policy. Labs were mandated to check for evidence of adulterants. The new law required testing of all urine samples, not just the suspicious ones. A positive adulterant result was worse for the participant than a positive drug test, because it amounted to fraud. The lab developed tests for adulterants, including Urine Luck.

Calvin couldn't wait until #32449's urine showed up in the lab again. Meanwhile, Jaco had gotten wind of these rule changes. He knew he had to stop using Urine Luck. "Now what am I going to do?" he asked his roommate. The stakes were higher. He'd stopped using marijuana and instead he was using heroin regularly now. Like most addicts, he had to have a hit almost daily and could not quit. He had also become the driver for the elementary school children. Unbeknownst to Calvin, his own daughter, Jenny, was one of Jaco's daily passengers.

Two months after the new drug testing regulation was in force, the results of #32449's urine appeared on Calvin's desk. It was positive for morphine, the heroin metabolite.

"We finally got him," Calvin said to me that day. "Now maybe he can be prosecuted accordingly."

I replied, "This is his first offense. He'll have an opportunity to defend himself. This is not over yet."

Jaco met with a medical review officer, or MRO. He explained that he'd had a clean toxicology record for ten years, and that this was all a big mistake. Jaco had seen a Seinfeld episode and remembered that Elaine had a positive urine result due to poppy seed ingestion, which contains morphine. He remarked in an innocent tone to the MRO, "I ate a poppy seed bagel yesterday. Could that have had any effect?"

The MRO responded, "Yes, poppy seeds are well known to contain morphine. I'm going to recommend that the bus

7

company put you on probation. From now on you'll have to submit to monthly drug tests and they'll be randomly scheduled. We will also arrange to have someone witness you urinating into a cup. You better clean up your act buddy, real fast."

Hearing the outcome of the MRO's hearing on #32449 and that he was only on probation, Calvin was livid. He became obsessed with trying to prove that #32449 was a drug addict. After a few days of research, he came across an article in a toxicology journal by researchers at the University of Connecticut. The investigators showed that testing urine for the presence of thebaine could be used to confirm poppy seed ingestion. Thebaine is not present in street heroin as it is not derived from the poppy plant. Excited, Calvin showed me the article and asked if the lab could test #32449's urine for thebaine.

"No Calvin," I replied. "You're getting too personally involved in this one case. If you don't drop this, you may face disciplinary action." But Calvin disobeyed. He did set up a test for thebaine and examined #32449's urine without my knowledge or permission. As he'd suspected, the result was negative, indicating that #32449 was lying about his positive test result.

I knew it, damn it, he said to himself. *He is a drug user.*

The next week, Jaco went to work driving the school bus. He had just taken a hit of heroin. It was a rainy day, and his vision was impaired. It didn't help that he was also in an opiate haze. He swerved across the center line and hit a woman and a child in their car head on. The children on the bus were thrown about. There were no seat belts. There were loud screams followed by crying. Miraculously, neither he nor any of the children on the bus were seriously hurt. The driver and passenger of the car, however, both died at the scene, their car crushed by the oncoming speeding bus.

Calvin heard the news on the radio and was horrified. The bus was carrying kids from Jenny's school. A chill ran down his spine. He frantically ran to his office to grab his cell phone to call home. Then he remembered that his wife had taken Jenny to the dentist and that Jenny was going to miss school. She was not on that bus. A crowd in the lab gathered in the break room where the news was being reported on local television. The station interrupted the regularly scheduled daytime soaps. A few minutes later, Calvin's cell phone, which was still in his hands, unexpectedly rang. It was from the police.

*

Testing for adulterants by forensic laboratories continues to evolve and improve in order to catch cheaters of the drug-testing system. Unfortunately, "garage" chemists also evolve by developing new adulterating agents that are designed to mask positive urine drug test results. Moreover, adulteration testing countermeasures add to the cost of testing the drugs themselves.

I believe there is a good deal of hypocrisy surrounding the federal workplace drug testing laws in the U.S. today. On one hand, drug use while working has its penalties. On the other, it is legal in many states for manufacturers to produce products purposely designed to allow someone to pass a drug test. The scope of testing is also incomplete. For example, the mandated testing for phencyclidine, or Angel Dust, makes little sense when the prevalence of this drug is so low. Meanwhile, the abuse of many other drugs, like oxycodone, goes on unabated. I realize that testing for a wide panel of drugs is impractical and costly. But improvements in testing policy must be made.

Accident Aftermath

****

Calvin was informed that his wife and family were in a terrible traffic accident. Their car was hit head on by a school bus. The driver and passenger, both belted in the car, died at the scene. In the damaged car, police officers found a purse and wallet belonging to Calvin's wife and identified her from the driver's license. Calvin's business card was also there with his work telephone number. The officer calmly told Calvin that their bodies were being taken to the medical examiner's office. He was then instructed to come to the ME's office within a few hours and identify his wife and child. The dieners at the morgue needed to clean up the bodies before Calving could see them.

Calvin came into my office and said he had to leave immediately. I did not know at the time but could sense that something terrible had happened. I went into the lab and assigned someone else to take over Calvin's duties. When I heard about a traffic accident with a bus from his coworkers, I suspected the worst.

Police officers arrived at the accident scene within a few minutes after the accident occurred. A witness who heard the screeching noise and loud crash dialed 9-1-1. When the police and medics arrived, they could see that Jaco was behaving erratically. Officers were trained to look for signs of physiological impairment and intoxication. Field sobriety tests were conducted. While standing, Jaco was instructed by an officer to lift one leg 6 inches above the ground and count out loud by thousands for 30 seconds. Jaco was unable to maintain his balance and he put his foot down after only 15 seconds. In the police report, the officer wrote, "Failed one leg standing test." With both feet on the ground, the policeman asked Jaco to focus on a pencil he held out in front of Jaco's eyes. The police officer slowly moved the pencil from side to side. He noticed that Jaco had difficulty tracking the moving pencil. Jaco's eyes jerked when the pencil moved 25 degrees from center. The officer wrote, "Failed the horizontal gaze nystagmus test." Based on these results, Jaco was put into the squad car and taken to the police station. There, a breathalyzer test was conducted. Jaco blew into the device which registered a 0.15%. This was nearly twice the legal limit for allowable alcohol consumption while operating a motor vehicle. The officers completed a report indicating that Jaco was legally drunk while operating the bus that day. They collected and blood and urine on Jaco and the samples were sent to the crime laboratory for analysis. He was read his rights and put into jail for the evening. Jaco did not have money to hire an attorney. A public defender was appointed to his case. A $100,000 bail was posted by his union and Jaco was released. A few days later, the results of the urine drug test were completed. Jaco's urine tested positive for 6-acetylmorpine and morphine. The drug testing laboratory indicated that these were heroin metabolites.

Based on these forensic findings, Jaco was charged with

driving while intoxicated for both alcohol and drugs, negligence, and involuntary manslaughter. His crime did not qualify as voluntary manslaughter because the act did not occur when he was provoked. The district attorney wanted to convict him of "criminally negligent" involuntary manslaughter because he was committing a reckless crime at the time of the accident. A key discussion between the DA and the defendant's lawyer was whether or not the defendant was aware of the risk. Jaco admitted that he abused drugs for many years and had a very clean driving record. Therefore he did not have a consciousness of risk.

"It was rainy that day and the roads were slick," the defending's attorney said. "In examining police records, I found several other accidents that occurred in the city."

"But none of them were due to heroin use and none resulted in the death of a woman and her young child," the DA argued.

The defense attorney argued that his client committed the "unlawful act" of manslaughter. "This was *malum prohibitum* and not *malum in se*" he said to the judge in his private chambers. The judge and DA knew the distinction, where in *Malum in se* the conduct is bad itself while *malum prohibitum*, the lesser of the two offenses, the conduct is bad because it is prohibited by law.

"My client did not foresee that his actions would be the direct cause of the accident. He was a competent driver and not any more negligent than usual. The major contributory factor was bad weather," the defense attorney concluded.

In the end, Jaco was convicted by a jury of his peers of the unlawful act of manslaughter for the death of Calvin's wife and daughter. He was given a 10-year sentence with probation after 7 years. This was a lesser sentence than what he would have received with negligent manslaughter.

Upon hearing this verdict, Calvin's co-workers at the lab were outraged. I, having testified in court many times, couldn't believe the outcome either.

"That creep should be locked up for the rest of his life," one of my techs said.

"What is the point of drug testing if someone can get off with this sentence," said another. I had no comment and left the break room.

*

Calvin was numbed by the sudden death of his entire family. The funeral was held that weekend. Calvin's parents and friends were in attendance. Some of the people from my lab were there. Many of his co-workers from the lab came. During the service, I sat at the back of the funeral home and paid my respects. I told Calvin to take off as much time as needed. He didn't respond. He had a blank stare on his face. The world that he knew had crumbled overnight. Little did I know then how much things would change?

A few days after the funeral, his family left town. Calvin was left alone in the home he and his wife built for themselves. The newspapers from the last few days were still in his driveway wrapped in plastic. He went outside to retrieve and discard them. But then he decided that while it was extremely painful for him, he wanted to see what the reporters said about the accident. He found the paper from the day after the accident in the metro section. There he read that the bus driver was being held for questioning by the police. Calvin then looked at each of the following days for further news.

The paper from four days after the accident read, "Lab tests showed that the Jaco Jamison was under the influence of drugs and alcohol at the time of the accident that killed a child and her mother. Mr. Jamison's employment as a bus driver for the Sunrise School District has been suspended pending a trial."

From his work, Calvin knew that all school bus drivers underwent regular urine drug testing. He then realized that his laboratory does the testing for the Sunrise District. *How could this driver be allowed to work if he abuses drugs?* Calvin thought to himself. *Drug testing is conducted to prevent hiring and using intoxicating drivers. So if he is on drugs, how could he be allowed to....* Then a chill through ran down his spine. *Maybe Jaco is Mr. #32449!* he thought. *Maybe he is the one who killed my family!*

Calvin was now determined at all costs to find out if Jaco was this donor of adulterated urine. He knew that all donors signed the first page of the original chain of custody documents each time they donate urine. The signature is not carried over to the subsequent copies, including the page that accompanies the sample to the laboratory. There was no way to find out who #32449 was from the toxicology lab's document. But Jaco knew the location of the urine collection station. Records identifying the donor would be locked in their files. So the next night, Calvin drove to the urine collection station after their closure. Calvin knew there were no watch guards on duty and no alarms in the building. Most people didn't know what goes on in this building. Calvin broke in through the office window and started looking through the files for the information he wanted. The files were listed numerically according to donor number. He found the drawer containing donors #32000 through #32500. With a few minutes, he found the file marked #32449 toward the back of the drawer. He was now sweating profusely. His heart started racing. His hand was shaking as he held the flashlight. Scanning down the form to the signature line, he found what he was looking for.

Calvin whispered out loud. "Donor #32449 is Jaco Jamison! This is the same man who murdered my family." Then Calvin thought he heard a noise from outside. He found what he was looking for so he quickly replaced the file into its rightful position, closed the file drawer and seeing no one, he left the building.

When he got home, Calvin starting thinking about this Jaco person. *The name sounds familiar,* he thought. Calvin saw that the newspaper reported that Jaco was 26 years old. *How do I know this name?* On a hunch, Calvin pulled out his old high school yearbook he bought when he was a freshman. Sure enough, Jaco Jamison went to the same high school and was a senior that year. Looking more closely at the picture and thinking back to his freshman year, jogged his memory. *He's the kid that pushed me in the bathroom! He was a creep even back then. I hope he gets life imprisonment for what he did to my family.*

The first thing in the morning of the next day, Calvin came back to the laboratory, barged into my office and slammed the door. The window of my office shook and nearly shattered under the concussion. I had never seen Calvin so enraged. He was always calm and quiet before.

"I know that donor #32449 was the bus driver who

killed my family," he shouted.

"Calvin, calm down. What are you talking about?" I responded.

"He is the donor of that urine sample that I found adulterated. Mr. 32449 killed my family," Calvin reiterated.

"How could you know that? This is confidential information. How did you get this information? You could be held libel...."

"Never mind how I know," Calvin interrupted. I could see he didn't care about any consequences to this breach of confidentiality. I found out and it's him. It's all your fault. I blame YOU for the death of my family. "

I was flabbergasted at hearing this rant. *How am I involved?* I asked myself. *What is he saying?*

"We knew this man was a menace to the public. You knew it too, and yet you did NOTHING to get him off the street." Calvin was shouting and crying at the same time. I had never seen this behavior from my former student and employee. "I wanted to report his positive drug test results and urine adulteration practices to the bus company, but you did not allow it. Now my wife and daughter are dead. I hope you go to hell for this!"

I felt about as small as a man could feel. I knew that he was right. We didn't report the result that could have led to Jaco's dismissal as a driver. As he was shouting, I thought of my own family. How devastated I would be if anything happened to them. But I also knew that if we had inappropriately reported this result, my laboratory could be sued, our work suspended, or the lab could have been forced to close. I myself could face criminal charges regarding breech of privacy. None of this knowledge made me feel any better. There was nothing I could say to Calvin to ease his pain. I got up from my desk and tried to reach for him, but he shoved me back.

"Stay away. I never want to see you again," he shouted. He then yelled some more obscenities at me and stomped out of the room. I didn't try to stop him as he left. Several of the lab workers were watching this drama take place. I could sense that many felt I was at fault. I shut the door, turned off the light in my office and sat at my desk in the dark with my head in my hands. *Maybe there could have been something I should have done*, I thought to myself. After 30 minutes, I got up and left the building. My staff was glaring at me as I left. I looked down the entire time and did not make any eye contact. I took sick days off for the remainder of that week.

Over the next few days, I was thinking about quitting my job as the toxicology lab director. I took a few more days off, but by the following week, I returned to the lab to resume my duties. Nobody ever brought up Calvin's case or wanted to discuss the death of his family after the funeral. About two weeks later, I received a letter from Calvin's attorney stating that effective immediately, his client was resigning his post in my laboratory. The attorney left instructions as to where his final paycheck was to be sent. I passed the letter on to our human resources office. The next day, that office posted a job opening to fill Calvin's position that was now vacant. I was not surprised that Calvin resigned. I hoped he could find peace with himself.

*

Calvin left town and flew to Barbados. He didn't tell

anyone where he was going or when or if he would return. Calvin was not an alcoholic and never drank heavily before. But now he needed something to forget about his troubles. He developed a taste for tequila and drank every night while he was away. He passed out in his room and slept for 14-18 hours. He would not wake up until late in the afternoon the following day. Calvin would eat something, but then start drinking heavily again. After a week of this behavior, he realized he had to stop and resume his life. But he had quit his job at my lab and he didn't know what to do or where to go. He couldn't live in the house that he and his wife had built. The memories were too painful. He planned to put his house on the market when he returned and move to a new city to start over. He needed a job as he was just 33 years old. But what was he going to do? He felt the clinical toxicology field let him down and he no longer valued it as a profession. Yet this was all that he knew. Calvin was sitting in the bar when someone approached him. The man sat down next to him and started a casual conversation. This chance meeting was going to change everything.

In order to make their plan work, they needed a biochemist. Someone who was smart and willing to work on products that were a little outside the norm. Since Calvin used to work for me, he remembered what happened to one of the graduate students that used to work in my department. Cao Pham was arrested for keeping anthrax in his lab shortly after the 9-1-1 attack. He left graduate school after his second girlfriend died a tragic death. From his old school, Calvin obtained Cao's contact information and asked if he was interested in joining Test-Me Inc. Cao had done some protein synthesis while in grad school and accepted the job.

*

A patient's medical information is protected by the Health Insurance Portability and Accountability Act (HIPAA) of 1996. There are stiff penalties and criminal charges that can be filed for individuals violating an individual's private information.   Although there are different interpretations that have been rendered, workplace urine drug testing is not considered medical information. Donors for drug testing are not patients and the testing is not conducted for diagnostic or medical purposes. Therefore most states have the prevailing view that drug test results are not PHI (protected health information) and HIPAA regulations do not apply. Nevertheless, there are other privacy laws that govern the release of workplace drug testing information and Calvin violated these laws.   As someone who was made aware of this violation, I was negligent in not reporting this breach in confidentiality. Given what Calvin went through, I was reluctant to report his indiscretion.   It was also unclear who I would report him to?   He was no longer my employee and the bus company had already discharged Jaco from his job and he was currently serving a prison sentence.

Mask

****

Barney Davis booked a one way trip to Barbados and flew in first class. He made $100,000 on his last job and could afford the trip. He ordered a mai tai from the flight attendant, reclined his seat as far back as it would go, and fell asleep on the way to the island. Barney was a professional con artist. He duped his last mark on a phony real estate deal. He showed him the sucker photos and a fake deed of land he owned in Arizona. "We're building a Casino and entertainment center on Indian land" he told him. Barney was a smooth talker, wore expensive clothes and drove a late model Bentley. The latter, of course, was rented. *It is a good thing he didn't Google map the address I gave him*, Barney thought to himself. He would have found it fifty miles out in the desert. Nothing but cactus out there.

As he sat by the pool, Barney was thinking about his next scam. Barney was staying at the same hotel as Calvin. The widower was sitting by the pool side bar, alone, and depressed. Barney studied him for the next half hour. Something terrible happened to this man he thought. He looks like he lost his last friend. Or his last dollar.

Curious to hear his story, Barney walked over and sat down next to Calvin.

"Hey pal, you look like you could use a friend. Buy you a

brew?" he said to Calvin.

"Get lost asshole," Calvin said without looking up.

"Hey, I meant no disrespect." Barney said. He was never one to push an issue, especially during the first contact. Barney started to get up to return to his lounger by the pool.

Calvin looked up and saw that Barney meant no harm. He said, "Look, I'm sorry. I didn't mean to snap at you. It has just been a rough week."

Barney saw that Calvin was about finished with a Corona so he signaled the bartender to bring two more bottles. This was followed by about two six packs as the evening wore on. Barney learned that Calvin's family was killed by someone who abused heroin, that he was a laboratory scientist, and that it was his own lab that let the drug abuser pass the drug test which kept him at a school bus driving job. Barney saw a lot of anger behind Calvin's sadness. Then Calvin told him that because of his obsession in catching Jaco's drug adulteration practices, Calvin was now an unrecognized expert on the subject of masking agents. He not only knew how the drug testing industry worked, but how the system could be beaten. Calvin also knew about changes to the drug testing policies that would enable drug testing laboratories to look for adulterants and catch urine adulterers like Jaco in the future. Implementation of these new testing policies would soon put Urine Luck and other similar adulterant products out of business. But there is room for a next generation of product that could escape detection.

Although he was a little drunk, Barney listened intently. He was getting tired of his real estate scam and believed that sooner or later he would get caught. He wanted to get into something more legitimate. He saw that Calvin really knew what he was talking about and was serious about producing these products. He told Calvin that "with my funding and your know-how, we can start a new company based on your scientific knowledge." Calvin was hesitant at first. He worked these last few years trying to catch cheaters. Now he was talking about facilitating cheaters on a grand scale.

Then Barney said, "You have nothing to feel bad about. The drug testing system failed you and your family so what do you have to lose?"

"Your right," Calvin said. "I owe them nothing. Let's do this."

Over the next several weeks, Barney and Calvin hired a lawyer and drew up papers for a limited liability corporation called "Test-Me, Inc." They leased a small warehouse and converted it into offices and a laboratory. They soon made plans for their first product. Calvin knew that the current adulterants contained chemicals called oxidizers, that react with the drug in a urine sample to form an entirely new compound that would then escape detection by the lab. Calvin learned that soon, the drug testing laboratory would be permitted by governmental regulations to test for the presence of these oxidants or bleaches. The new lab detection scheme procedure involves adding an indicator that changes color in the presence of the adulterant in the urine sample. *What can I do to beat this system?* Calvin thought. He needed to find a compound that can quickly react with a drug in a sample soon after it is added to the urine, and then stop working. When the urine is tested a day or so later, the adulteration indicator reaction performed by the lab would fail and the urine sample would produce a negative result. Calvin did some more reading and came up with a plan. There are enzymes called "peroxidases" that are capable of oxidizing drugs. Enzymes are proteins found throughout nature that facilitate chemical reactions. In the lab, Calvin knew that most enzymes only work under precise conditions. One of those is the pH or the hydrogen ion concentration in the urine. The normal pH is about 7. Calvin found a peroxidase that worked best at a pH just above this value. When he added it to a urine sample containing cocaine, he found that the enzyme was initially reactive towards cocaine. But after a few minutes, the enzyme itself becomes non-functional. But by then, however, the enzyme has done its job. Calvin found a new way to beat the current testing system for detecting adulterants! He asked Barney to hire a programmer to construct a website and within a month, Test-Me was producing a product and they were taking orders for this new adulterant. They called it "Mask." Soon, word got around that Mask not only works but escapes detection. He was selling thousands of vials and making hundreds of thousands of dollars out of his garage. Within a few months, they had money to lease an office and lab. They hired more people to keep up with the demand.

*

As part of my job as the clinical toxicology lab director, I got word of the existence of Mask within a few months after its release. I did not know or could even dream that my former student was behind this product. I asked one of my graduate students to purchase Mask from the internet and we went about studying how it worked. It didn't take us long to realize that the active ingredient was an enzyme. We constructed a test that could be used to detect the presence of the peroxidase adulterant. But we could not justify the added cost of testing this adulterant for all urine samples we received each day. At the time, we just hoped that this product would not get widely used. Unbeknownst to us, this became a potentially important issue during a routine drug analysis of a donor's urine..........

*

Ralph majored in inorganic chemistry as an undergraduate in college and became a research technician under Dr. Kate Vetter, a chemistry professor at the city college. Dr. Vetter was studying how the exposure to heavy metals causes illnesses by interrupting the ability of DNA to repair itself. Ralph had used marijuana throughout college but he never had a urine test before. In order to get a job in the lab, he was told to donate urine for a pre-employment drug test. This was a new and controversial program that was just instituted at the school a month ago. There were many protests by students and faculty. Ralph was one of them. But in his case, it wasn't because of any civil rights violations. Ralph was not politically active. It was only because he was a drug abuser and didn't want to stop. Ralph wanted this job and knew his urine would be positive for several weeks. So even if he stopped using for a few days, his urine would remain positive. So Ralph went on line and found an ad about Mask.

"This is specially formulated to escape detection by current testing procedures in use in all forms of drug testing," Ralph read, "Developed by a toxicologist with 10 years of experience working in a drug testing facility." Ralph was convinced Mask would work for him. He mailed in a certified check for $59.99, and paid extra to have Mask sent by express mail. The product arrived the next day to his home address in an unlabeled brown envelope.

On the day of the drug test, Ralph was given a specimen cup and instructed to produce a urine sample. He was alone in the restroom. There was no sink in the bathroom and the toilet water was blue. After filling the cup with urine, Ralph removed the vial of Mask and emptied the contents into the urine cup. He screwed on the orange cap and swirled the mixture. He then left the bathroom giving the sample to the collector. Only then was he allowed to wash his hands using the sink outside the bathroom. Ralph signed the necessary papers and left the station. Let's hope this works or I will have to go elsewhere for a job, Ralph thought. A few days later, he got a call from the University's human resources office saying that he had passed the drug test and Dr. Vetter was ready to hire him. The following week, Ralph was on the job.

During the next several months, Ralph was trained on the use of nuclear magnetic resonance spectroscopy or NMR. In the medical world, this technique is also known as magnetic resonance imaging or "MRI" and it is an important tool for visualizing organs and tumors. Dr. Vetter was using NMR for characterizing inorganic compounds. Ralph was trained to use dimethylmercury to calibrate the instrument.

"Be extremely careful when using this compound," Dr. Vetter told him. "Make sure you wear a double layer of gloves when handling this solution."

Blah, blah blah, Ralph thought to himself. She is being overly cautions. I have played with mercury when I accidently broke a mercury-filled thermometer at home. I never had any problems. As a liquid metal, mercury has some very peculiar physical properties that can be fun to play with for a child. It forms droplets that roll across surfaces. The metal is very shiny. What Dr. Vetter failed to mention to Ralph that while elemental mercury is dangerous, the organic form of metal is much more toxic.

Ralph was instructed to calibrate the NMR instrument one day when he was alone in the lab. He was feeling a little depressed so he took a break and went outside to smoke a joint. When he returned, he was in a much better mood. However, his pot was somewhat hallucinogenic and his perception was altered. He took a pipette containing dimethylmercury and filled the calibration chamber of the instrument. When completed, he went to discard the pipette, but without knowing it, he accidently spilled a small drop of the solution onto the instrument's keyboard. It fell onto the "3" key near the top left, just below the top row of the function keys. Ralph performed the experiment that was needed on the instrument. When the study was done, he called Dr. Vetter to review the results. She was not in the office so he left her a message saying that the results were ready for her to review. Ralph had to leave early but knew that Dr. Vetter would return later that day, because she had told him that this was an important analysis.

The droplet settled onto the cradle of the key. There it dried to a colorless residue. The room was dark. Only the light from the monitor was on. On the key rested the poison, undisturbed. The professor returned from her afternoon meeting and saw the message light on her office phone and listened to Ralph's comments. It was after 6:00 pm and she was tired. Should I look at the data now or wait until tomorrow? The evening custodial staff had just arrived and was beginning to make their rounds. She decided she would go and take a quick look at the data. She went into the lab, turned on the lights, and sat at the keyboard. She logged onto the terminal and began typing in the commands she needed to access the data. Looking at her notes, she typed in the sample number and with her right hand, using the numbers keypad to the right of the main letters on the keyboard. She hit enter but the computer terminal responded as "sample not found." Then she remembered that she had to enter the number sign. So she hit the shift key with her index finger on her right hand and hit the 3 key with her middle finger of her left hand. She was not wearing any gloves. Why would she? She was sitting at a computer terminal. But without her knowledge, she was exposed to the methylmercury from the dried residue. The poison seeped through the tip of her finger. She felt nothing and went about her work. When she saw the final data, she sat back in her chair satisfied that the study was conducted correctly and the conclusion she wanted was verified. She logged off the terminal, and left the lab to go home. She would have dinner alone, take a bath and read a few chapters in the book by her bedside before retiring.

The next 9 months did not go well for Dr. Vetter. She initially suffered diarrhea and a 6 pound weight loss. Her doctors thought she had cancer. A series of laboratory and radiology tests including CT and MRI scans were ordered. Nothing came up positive. Dr. Vetter then developed tingling in her fingers and saw brief flashes of light. This changed the focus of her medical examination and she was referred to an occupational medicine specialist, Dr. Kaylani Washington.

"What type of research do you do?" Dr. Washington

asked.

"I characterize inorganic chemicals and complexes containing cadmium," was her response.

"So you are exposed to cadmium on a regular basis?"

"I am not directly exposed, my research lab assistant performs the studies that I plan. I am involved with data analysis only," Dr. Vetter stated.

"I am going to order blood and urine tests to see if by somehow you were exposed to this metal."

The samples came to my toxicology laboratory for testing. At that time, we used a technique called atomic absorption spectroscopy. The sample was prepped and the analysis took a few hours to run. When completed, the result was within the normal limits. I reported the negative result to Dr. Washington who was disappointed.

"I was sure this was the cause of her neuropathy," she said.

"We're obligated to test only what was ordered. We do have a new instrumental technique called an inductive-coupled mass spectrometer, that can look for the presence of all major heavy metals. In our previous method, only one metal can be tested at a time. We are still studying the performance of this instrument but if you order a compressive heavy metal screen, we can retrieve Dr. Vetter's samples and run them."

"Let's do it" Dr. Washington said.

The ICP method produced a mercury level that was 250 times the normal limit. The urine concentration was 50 times normal. The investigation of her work environment showed that methylmercury was used as a calibrator. Dr. Vetter's mental recall had deteriorated to the extent that she forgot to mention their use of this metal. The professor was placed on chelation therapy and new samples were sent to my laboratory for retesting a month later. The result came out a thousand fold higher than the previous high result. My lab tech was astonished to see this new result.

"Is she getting worse?" he asked.

"No, this is actually a good thing," I responded to him. This means that the chelator is removing the drug from her body. But was the treatment started too late?"

It was. Kate Vetter died of methylmercury poisoning 13 months after her being poisoned. How she got exposed was never determined. On the night of her poisoning, the evening janitorial crew sprayed the countertops with ammonia. They also cleaned the keyboards with a cleaning spray. Nobody else got exposed to the dimethylmercury. Had Dr. Vetter decided to go home instead of work that day, she would not have been exposed either.

Counseling services were held for her grieving students The University had a memorial service for her. The funding of Dr. Vetter's research lab ended with her passing. Ralph lost his job as a research technician. He joined another lab never knowing that it was his careless action that caused his former boss' death. The following year, the Kate Vetter Endowed Chair of DNA Mutagenesis was named in her honor, and a new faculty member was recruited to fill the void she left.

*

In 1996, Dr. Karen Wetterhahn was a professor of chemistry at Dartmouth College when she accidently exposed herself to dimethylmercury. While performing an experiment, just two drops of the compound fell on to her glove and seeped into her skin. Within a few months, Dr. Wetterhahn developed neurological symptoms including loss of balance, loss of speech and a reduced ability to write. As a scientist, these are essential skills needed to perform studies, write observations, and publish papers. She was admitted to the Massachusetts General Hospital where she was treated with vitamin E and succimer and exchange transfusions to reduce her body burden of mercury. Her condition continued to spiral downward. Toward the end, she entered a vegetative state with spontaneous episodes of agitation and crying. She died around 300 days after her exposure.

As shown in this case, dimethylmercury is extremely dangerous. Dr. Wetterhahn's death lead to changes in safety practices surrounding the use of this metal and other hazardous metals. Latex gloves provide insufficient protection against spills from these chemicals. The use of chemical resistant gloves has made research in this area safer, but the risks are still present.

Workplace drug testing continues to be an important deterrent to drug abuse. Drug testing programs have expanded from federal employees to the private sector. The Substance Abuse and Mental Health Services Administration, who regulate drug testing laboratories continue to upgrade their program. For example, they have lowered the cutoff concentration for cocaine and amphetamine and have added 6-monoacetylmorpine and Ecstasy to the menu of tests. They have also permitted the collection and testing of oral fluids. This latter action is a major advancement in the fight against adulterants. An individual is not likely to put a caustic chemical in their mouth prior to oral fluid collection. Unlike urine, where the donor voids in the privacy of a bathroom stall, the collection of oral fluids is performed in the presence of the collector. Therefore, oral fluid collection while more analytically difficult for the testing laboratory, has likely lowered the rate of false negative detection among drug abusers.

The Prosthetic

****

John and Nancy watched the horrible proceedings as they unfolded on their television set.

"This is worse than any fictional story we could come up with" John told his wife. The media people were talking about one of their own hometown boys. Someone they had a hand in molding into what he eventually who he would become. They lived in a small town. Nobody had ever been on the national news before. Not like this.

"How could it have come to this?" Nancy cried.

*

Organized youth football in America began in Philadelphia in 1929, when the owner of a factory wanted to organize an activity to occupy children in the neighborhood to prevent them from throwing rocks and breaking windows in his factory. In 1934, the league was named after Glen Scobey "Pop" Warner, the college football coach who won several college national championships. Today, Pop Warner Little Scholars is a football, cheerleading and dance program serving about a half million American youths between the ages of 6 and 15 years.

Harold Millner played in Pop Warner Football in a small

town outside of Houston. It was clear to everyone watching that he was the best player on the field. When he was in high school, his team won the state championship in the 5A division of schools with student enrollments of between 1060 and 2099 pupils. Harold played both on defense as a defensive back, and offense where he was the fullback. There were no other players that could match Harold's physical stature of six foot five inches and 245 pounds of pure muscle. Harold could also run the 40 yard dash in 4.7 seconds, a time as good as many professional football players.

Harold got a full scholarship to attend Texas State University, the premiere school in the state. It is extremely rare for someone to play both offense and defense in college, so his coaches told him that they were going to make him a full time linebacker. This was his best position and he did not argue against it. Harold made the starting line up during his freshman year. Many of the other incoming freshman football players were "red shirted" by the coaches. That enabled these student-athletes to get adjusted to the rigors of academic life, living away from home, and get experience to the speed and power of the college game. The coaches saw that Harold was too valuable a player to be red-shirted. Academic life for Harold was difficult because his reading comprehension was only at the 8th grade level. While his teachers in high school tried to get him to study, they were often overruled by his coaches.

"Harold's future won't be found in them books," commented John, one of his coaches, to his wife Nancy, a guidance counselor at the same school. "He will be a professional ballplayer and we cannot stand in his way."

"What if he gets hurt and cannot play? We owe it to him to give him an education so he has a fighting chance to succeed if something happens to him in football" Nancy replied.

"Have you seen him on Friday nights?" referring to the local fall football games. "There isn't anyone who is going to take him down."

Now in college, the coaches arranged a curriculum of courses that suited Harold's capabilities. This included classes in physical education, auto-mechanics, and the wood shop. Harold was good with his hands. He was also pretty good in art and sculpture. Many of his classmates wanted him to be a male model for their sculpture, because his physique was like that of a Greek god. Harold was not embarrassed to show off his body. In the locker room, he was used to having other players look at him while he was in the shower or getting dressed. They weren't gay, they just marveled at this modern day Adonis.

In the first college game, Harold made 13 tackles against a lesser non-conference opponent. At that time, there was no national championship game in college, so the best team in the country was decided through polls of writers and coaches. Therefore, many strong teams would play host to a low ranking division I-A school or a division I-AA school, and win by large scoring margins. Texas State won by a large margin. Although the school did not win the conference during his freshman year, Harold was an immediate standout and made the All-Conference team. By the end of his senior year, Texas State won two conference championships. Harold was on the Sports Illustrated All-American Team in each of his last two years. As a senior, he was a finalist for the Heisman Trophy Award for the best college player. Harold was at the Downtown Athletic Club in New York City for the ceremony where the quarterback from the University of Southern California was announced as the winner. Harold finished second. He knew that most award winners were either quarterbacks or running backs.

A few weeks after the NFL season, Harold was preparing for the NFL draft of college football players. He had dropped out of school without getting a degree and hired an agent. This was part of his master plan all along. He never thought it was valuable for him to complete college. He read the newspaper reports that stated that he would likely be either the first or second player chosen that year. This was going to be a large payday for him. Harold had focused on football every year since his Pop Warner days. The linebacker didn't have to wait long. The New York Spartans, who had the first pick, called Harold's agent and told him they were going to select his client first.

On draft day, Harold was back in New York City but this time at Madison Square Garden where the draft was being held. John and Nancy were home in Texas watching the proceedings on television.

The NFL commissioner stepped up to the microphone and announced, "With the first pick of the 2001 NFL draft, the New York Spartans picked Harold Millner, linebacker, Texas State University." As Harold was walking onto the stage, someone gave him a Spartans hat to put on. Once he was in front of the audience, he shook hands with the Commissioner, who gave him a New York Spartans jersey with his last name already sewn onto the back.

"I told you he would make it big," John told Nancy.

"I still think we did him a disservice by not educating him," she replied.

"He doesn't have to worry, his payday has arrived."

Calvin was not watching the program as he was not a sports fan and knew nothing about pro football. I on the other hand, felt that a future pro football hall of famer was being introduced.

Within a few weeks, Harold signed a lucrative multi-year contract and began his pro career as a Spartan. Like during his college days, Harold was a standout on the team. But the Spartans were rebuilding their team around Harold and other key players, and it would be several years before they became competitive with the other teams in the league.

In 1987, the NFL instituted a policy against the use of performance enhancing drugs including anabolic steroids. All players and coaches were subjected to random testing of urine during the season and the off season. The league recognized that steroids were being increasingly used among their players. They recognized that the playing field was no longer level, and feared that college and even high school players would resort to using these supplements just to compete.

Harold underwent regular drug testing throughout his college career so he was familiar with the NFL's program. Harold did not use PEDs. He knew that his skills as a football player were natural and God given. So Harold passed each and every test.

*

Unlike Calvin, Barney was a big sports fan. He had four season ticket seats to the professional team in town and went to all their games. Barney and his friends would tailgate in the parking lot before and after each game. It became a fall Sunday afternoon ritual when the team was at home. Because of his interest in the team, Barney convinced Calvin that there was a market for a new product designed for professional athletes.

"I don't understand, Barney. Isn't the collection of athletes witnessed? How can someone adulterate their urine if it is collected in plain view of the collector at all times?"

"We make an artificial penis," Barney said calmly. "We fill it with drug free urine. The donor places it over their real penis. When it comes time to urinate, he squeezes a button hidden underneath the shaft that discharges the pressurized fluid from a reservoir and out the tip. We can make it look like a real urine flow."

"Hold on, men have different lengths and color. How do we..."

Barney interrupted Calvin in mid-sentence. "Jocks generally have larger dicks than the normal guy. We can customize the size and color to match the athlete. Sort of like a designer dong."

"I think you're off your wiener on this one but if you want to do this, go ahead and produce a prototype. But I am not going to be a model," Calvin said as he left the room.

*

Harold lived up to the large contract he signed as a rookie. Just like everybody predicted, Harold made the Pro-Bowl in eight of his first ten years. Over the course of a single season, he led the league in sacks 6 times and had the most interceptions once. His team got into the playoffs in this third year and won the Super Bowl in the eighth year. He was a shoo-in to be a Hall of Famer once he decided to retire. His notoriety was further heightened because he played in New York. Even during the off season, his exploits and conquests were well chronicled in the media. During the middle of his tenth season, Harold suffered a tear in both his anterior cruciate ligament and medial collateral ligament. During the play, he was chop-blocked. An offensive lineman hit him low planting his left knee and the tight end hit him high causing a tear in his ligaments. After it happened, he rolled onto his back holding his knee and screaming in agony. He was carried off the field, and taken to the hospital where doctors performed knee surgery. Today, that play would result in a 15-yard penalty but back then it was a legal play. Harold missed the remainder of the season and the playoffs. During his recovery, team doctors prescribed nandrolone decanoate, an anabolic steroid. The league was informed of this treatment. So long as he held an active medical prescription for the steroid, he would not fail a drug test.

Harold's doctors told him that he might not be able to play during the next season. This was a serious injury and many other players required more than a year to recover, while others athletes simply retired. Harold underwent rigorous physical therapy in hope of playing as well as he had before the injury. Football was everything in his life. And now that he was in his early thirties, he felt that he wasn't going to be as strong or as fast as before. Just before the start of spring training, Harold made plans to return to practice. His doctors had taken him off steroids, but secretly, he continued to use them. He felt that his performance would decline if he stopped using them. A former college teammate supplied him with the amount he needed. Harold learned from his doctor on how to inject himself with the juice.

Knowing that sooner or later he would be facing a urine drug test, he went online to find a way to cheat the testing NFL's surveillance system. I just need them to get me through training camp, he thought to himself. I won't use them during the regular season.

With the help of his girlfriend, Jasmine, they found what they were looking for. Pee Defender. This was an artificial device that fit over his own penis. Hidden underneath was a tube attached to a liquid reservoir. The pouch is filled with certified drug free urine that is purchased separately, and is designed to fit under the scrotum and between the legs. A diagram was provided to show how the pouch is hidden from view. The thin tubing is dark and also is nestled within the man's pubic hair. The reservoir is pressurized so that a stream is produced upon release of the valve. The objective is to provide a clean urine sample. The contraption is carefully disguised so that unless the witness is observing very closely, it appears that the individual is voiding his own urine. Harold purchased Pee Defender and urine which arrived the next day. With the help of his girlfriend, he installed the product and gave it a whiz. After a bit of practice, he became a whiz at it. He was now ready for the drug test that was sure to come.

Harold got the call to come to the donation center during the middle of the first week of training camp. The linebacker had all of the equipment he needed with him hidden in the duffle bag in his locker. Harold went into the stall to assemble the device and then went to the center. Thomas was assigned to collect urine from Harold. He was a big fan of the team and Harold in particular. In order to distract him, Harold engaged him in light conversation.

As he was pulling down his pants, Harold said to Thomas,

"So what do you think of the new crop of rookies we drafted?"

"That running back from Penn State looks really good," Thomas remarked. As he was speaking, Harold pulled Pee Defender out from his underpants and took the clean and empty cup from Thomas. He pushed the release valve from under the device and soon a stream of urine began flowing out of the device and into the container. Thomas was standing to the side of Harold and saw that the cup was filling up with urine. He did not suspect anything amiss and didn't know that the urine was not Harold's.

"I love hazing rookie tailbacks," Harold continues. "They all think they are going to be the next Emmitt Smith but I always give them a nice 'welcome to the NFL' greeting." Thomas knew that Harold would put the runner flat on his back during one the very first scrimmages.

Harold completed the donation and gave the filled cup to Thomas. The collector examined the temperature strip affixed to the cup to verify that the urine was within the acceptable temperature range. Harold had pre-warmed the drug-free sample by having it between his legs. Having passed the temperature check, Thomas then took the cup with his gloved hands and poured half of the urine into a second cup, and screwed the lids back onto both cups. Harold was watching while at the same time, pulling up his pants and zippering his fly. After washing his hands, Harold was asked to verify the information on the requisition form and to sign the paperwork. He also signed two strips of adhesive tape that had the same accessioning number as the requisition form. Thomas peeled off the strips one by one and placed them over the lid of each urine cup, one labeled "A" and the other cup labeled "B." Harold inspected the seal to ensure that it was intact.

If the seal is broken at any time, Harold knew that the test would be invalid and a repeat urine collection would be necessary. He didn't want to repeat this charade more than absolutely needed. Harold said to Thomas as he was departing, "I hope you make it to some of our games."

Me too, Thomas thought, knowing full well that the ticket prices were beyond his economic means.

*

As expected, Pee Defender enabled Harold to pass the test. He was cleared by his doctors to play that season. Harold continued to use nandrolone. The steroids made Harold stronger and more aggressive than ever before. It also allowed for a faster recovery after a workout, meaning that he could train for longer hours. All of the coaches noticed a new resolve in their star linebacker. They believed that having missed much of the last season was the reason for his renewed motivation. Nobody suspected that it was modern pharmacology that was responsible. The Spartans got off to a good start that season, easily beating the previous year's Super Bowl champ. The next game was with New England, their long-time conference rival. Harold really wanted to beat them because his injury last year occurred against this team. So he doubled up the steroid dose that week in hopes of being even more aggressive. The linebacker coach told him that he needed to take the opposing quarterback out. Harold knew what that meant. Harold had three sacks and one forced fumble of the opposing team's quarterback. During one sack, Harold heard the bone crunch of his hit on the quarterback's shoulder. The QB left the game and did not return. The Spartans revenged their loss from last season.

Harold was riding on a high in the locker room and was still on an emotional high when he got home. But when he arrived, he was surprised to see that Jasmine had another man in the apartment with her. They were in the dining room with coffee mugs, and books and papers scattered about.

"This is Ted," she said to him. Jasmine was still in school and she and Ted were studying together for a big exam. Harold had never met Ted before this night.

"It is a thrill to meet you sir. Great game today. We were watching as we were studying," Ted said. Harold towered over the student.

"Who the hell are you? What are you doing here? Get the fuck out."

"Harold! We're just studying," Jasmine said. But Harold would have nothing of it and made a move toward the boy.

"I'll call you later," Ted said as he was gathering his things to leave. As he was walking out the door, he could hear a loud argument taking place. Harold was in a rage and shouting at Jasmine. This hastened Ted's pace.

Jasmine knowing that she did nothing wrong made the mistake of fighting back. She didn't realize that Harold was not in control of his faculties and with his size and strength, he was a human weapon.

"Don't be talking to me like that, Harold Millner! I ain't done nothing wrong," she said.

This made Harold even more angry. Soon, he wasn't seeing his girlfriend, only an adversary. He got down on a three point stance and attacked her. He hit her hard in her shoulder pushing her straight into the wall. Harold heard the bone crunch of he hit his girlfriend. The force of the collision broke her collar bone. But unlike a quarterback, she was not a trained professional athlete. Her head hit the wall and snapped her neck. She fell into a motionless heap. Harold stood over the quarterback and shouted. "Not in my house!" Then he realized that it was his girlfriend who he hit and not the opposing team. "Oh my god! Jasmine, are you alright?" He picked up her lifeless head and feared the worst. He called 9-1-1 for help but it was too late. By the time they arrived, she was dead.

The police were called immediately and Harold was held for questioning. When the medical examiner saw that the girl's shoulder and neck were broke, Harold was taken into custody. He was charged with voluntary manslaughter. Harold's lawyer posted bail and he was remanded to the attorney's custody. The NFL and the New York Spartans suspended Harold with pay pending the outcome of the case. A few months later, a grand jury indicted him. During his trial, Ted was called to testify. He described the events leading up to Jasmine's death. Harold's coaches were subpoenaed and reluctantly testified in court. The district attorney showed films of the game that night and asked the defensive coordinator if Harold was acting overly aggressive that day. There was one play where he pushed aside three different 300 pound offensive linemen on route to the quarterback. When the passer was knocked down, Harold stood over his prize shouting at him, "Not in my house!" The coach simply stated that Harold's actions were within the acceptable limits of the game.

Against his lawyer's advice, Harold took the stand in hopes of getting some sympathy from the jury. But with his normal exemptions, the DA specifically eliminated potential jurists if they stated that they were fans of football. Harold admitted that he was using nandrolone for his knee rehabilitation. He didn't mean to hurt Jasmine. It was the steroids that made him go crazy that night. When asked how he passed the drug test, he told them about Pee Defender. He described in court exactly how he was able to pass the test, and he stated that many other NFL players were on juice and cheating by one means or another. "But none of them killed their wife or girlfriend" the district attorney said in his closing argument to the jury. Harold was sentenced to 8 years in prison. His NFL career was over in one brief instance of rage. Harold was eligible for the NFL's Hall of Fame while he was still in prison. While the dominant defensive player of his era, he never received any communication from the nominating committee.

*

After the telecast, John sat back from the set and turned it off with the remote. "You were right all along dear. We failed to put the proper values on this boy." Nancy did not feel any better, but could have said, *I told you so.*

*

Domestic violence has become a major issue among professional athletes, but especially among the NFL. The Commissioner has instituted new policies against offenders. There is no official link between performance enhancing drugs and these acts of violence. Likewise, there are no reported homicides or deaths linked to PEDs from an active player. Recently, the NFL suspended coaches for telling their players to purposely hurt the opposing team. The Commissioner has stated that while injuries are a major part of the game, a purposeful intent to harm is not in the game's best interest.

In his autobiography, Lawrence Taylor, the celebrated linebacker for the New York Giants admitted to using cocaine during the season. He passed urine drug tests by the substitution of clean urine from a teammate. But he was caught twice and suspended for several games. Since a third failed drug would have ended his career, Taylor stopped abusing cocaine until after his retirement.

Nandrolone is one of many anabolic steroids abused by athletes. These steroids are known to increase strength, endurance, muscle mass, and aggression. Among the notable athletes who tested positive include Petra Korda of professional tennis, Linford Christie, 1992 Olympic Gold Medalist and an unproven accusation by Brian McNamee about baseball pitcher Roger Clemens.

There is a commercial product available called the Whizzinator. Like the fictitious Pee Defender, it too comes in different colors to match the skin of the donor. Health professionals involved with witnessed urine drug collection should be educated to the existence of this twin.

Whippet!

It seemed unusual to Clara that her teenage son, Keith, would purchase so much whipped cream when he didn't even like deserts. One day, she confronted him about his behavior.

"What are you doing with all this whipped cream?" she asked her son. "There are always several cans of this in our refrigerator."

"I don't like pies, but my friends do," Keith responded. "They enjoy eating sweets after a practice session." Keith was the lead guitarist and singer in their rock band that they called "*Toxic Bland*". They practiced every day after school in Frank's family garage. Frank was the group's drummer. "We split up the costs. Frank buys the sweets and I buy the toppings. It is not always whipped cream, sometimes I get strawberries. The other guys chip in by buying beer and pretzels."

"Keith, you know I don't approve of drinking," his mother said.

"I am almost 18. Dad told me that he was drinking when he was my age," Keith said. In Wisconsin, the minimum age for drinking alcohol was 19 in 1986. "We live in Milwaukee. You can't tell me all of the other teenagers don't drink."

"I know I can't stop you boys, but I hope you do not drive while drinking," Clara said.

"Don't worry, mom, we always have a designated driver," Keith said. It was all a lie to get his mother to stop bothering him. Clearly, he was not using whipped cream for deserts. *I am moving out of the house next year when I graduate from high school.* He thought. *Then I won't have to put up with this crap.*

*

It was one the simplest and most profitable products that Calvin and Test-Me, Inc. could ever produce. First, his laboratory buys large canisters of the compressed gas. Then they acquire a set of small 2-inch evacuated aluminum canisters. A vacuum manifold fits over all of the small tubes, and a needle punctures the seal of these bottles. When the regulator is turned to the "on" position, gas from the large bottle simultaneously fills each of the small canisters. The manifold is removed, and a secondary seal is placed over each canister. They are now full and ready for sale.

The individual canisters called "chargers" contain a foil seal that releases gas when punctured. The product sold for $50 through online for a box of 48 chargers. Calvin had a contest at the office to see who could come up with the best name for the product. Samples were given to several of the employees, who wanted to try them at home. The following week, a single and very attractive secretary came up with the best name based on her personal experience with the product. She suggested "Enhance" because of the physiologic effect that it had when she used it. No further details were given regarding the circumstance by which she used it, but there were some snickers behind her back from some of the male workers. It was agreed that this would be the name on the outer box for their new product.

"Shouldn't we also label each individual canister?" Cao, the senior scientist asked Calvin.

"No, our customers will know what is inside and would prefer that the product not be labeled," Calvin said. A page was added to their website advertising this product. The gas was sold "for cooking and baking purposes." But everyone at Test-Me, Inc. knew who was purchasing these canisters and how they were really using it.

*

After graduation, Keith moved out of the family home and he and his friend Frank found an apartment in town. Keith got a job working in a music store. Frank, Keith, and the rest of the band spent all of their free time composing new music, practicing, and performing. They started at high school dances and private parties. Word soon got out that they were good, and *Toxic Bland* started to get bigger gigs on weekends. Within a few years, the group was making demo CDs for local distribution and sale. Keith peddled some of their music to the local stations hoping that their music would be played on the radio. One disc jockey, a "Mr. Groove," took a particular liking to their style. He started playing their songs on a regular basis on his afternoon program. Soon, *Toxic Bland* was invited to perform at regional venues in Madison, Chicago and Minneapolis.

The big break for *Toxic Bland* occurred following a bus accident when several members of another band were seriously injured. They were scheduled to be the opening act for an established touring rock band. Groove was called to see if he knew of a local group who could substitute at the last minute. He immediately called Keith and asked if they were available. Keith and his group jumped at the chance.

"This could be the break we need," he told Frank. All of the members took sick leave or quit their day jobs to practice hard every day for the next several weeks. There were lots of "canisters" consumed during these weeks. Their hard work paid off. The audience loved their performance at the BMO Harris Bradley Center in town. They even asked for an encore, which briefly annoyed the lead singer of the main act who followed. The following day, there was a review in the entertainment section of the local newspaper. Their appearance was described as being "refreshing, original, and stimulating." Soon, Keith started getting calls from people wanting to be their agent. After a few visits, they agreed that Groove, who didn't want the job at first, would be the most logical choice.

With Groove's help, *Toxic Bland* was asked to compose their first complete CD. Keith and Frank went to work writing original music and scripts to complete their repertoire. It took 9 months of work and another 3 months of daily rehearsal. Approximately one year after their breakout show, *Toxic Blend* had their first album. Grove and *Toxic Blend* had to decide if they were going to try to get one of the big "record" companies to distribute their album or to "self-release" their work. After discussing all of the pros and cons to both approaches, they settled on self-publication and distribution.

"Without a record company behind you, it will be difficult to get the public to hear your songs. I can do what I can at the radio station, but the best way is to schedule concerts. It will be a lot of traveling but this may be the best way." They all agreed with Groove. They were young, unmarried, and had boring jobs. It was their dream to be rock stars.

The climb to the top was slow and arduous. But their music was catching on. Soon, they were ready for a second album. They stopped touring for a while and Keith and Frank got busy writing again. Two years later, they released their next album. Most of the people who bought the first album were eager to hear their latest work. Soon, *Toxic Blend* was no longer an opening act but a headlining one. Their childhood dreams had come true. Their band was becoming a household name with a number of recognizable songs.

Rock and roll fame had its benefits and detractions. Young girls threw themselves at the band members trying to get their attention. Keith was the most popular because he was the lead singer and composer for most of their work. The band had more than their share of parties, drugs, alcohol, and sex.

Connie was one of the girls who became obsessed with Keith. She grew up on small farm nearby. She did not want to follow the path of her older brothers and sisters who married people who lived in the same town. She had both of the group's CDs and listened to their songs on the radio. When she heard that *Toxic Blend* was coming to the University of Wisconsin, she bought a ticket and together with her girlfriend Cynthia, they went to see them. Connie got all decked out in a see-through blouse that exposed her breasts. She stood in the front row of the mosh pit hoping to attract Keith's attention. Her plan worked. Keith's eyes were glued to her eyes as he played while she was dancing to his music. During a break, he asked Groove to pass

Connie a note that he signed. The note contained the name of the hotel where they were staying and the room number. Keith asked that she meet him there right after the show. Connie was thrilled when she received the note. She showed it to Cynthia and told her that she should go on home without her.

"How are you getting home tonight?" Cynthia wanted to know.

"Don't worry about me," Connie said. "I have big plans for tonight. Can you call my mom and say that I am staying over at your house?"

"But that's a lie. I am uncomfortable with this. What if something happens?" Cynthia asked.

"Nothing is going to happen. I'll be fine. Can you do this once for me? Or maybe you can come join us, it will be a lot of fun." Connie really threw caution to the wind.

"No way I'm doing that. I'll cover for you this one time. You better not get into trouble," Cynthia said as they drove to the hotel and Cynthia left her there.

Connie waited an hour in the hotel lobby for the group to arrive after they closed the show. Keith saw Connie from a distance and winked. Connie waited another 15 minutes and then got into the elevator and headed for Keith's suite. She knocked on the door and was greeted by Groove. "Come on in" he said to the girl. Keith was standing by the bar drinking scotch. He came over and gave her a big hug.

"Did you like the show?" he asked her but wasn't really interested in her answer.

"I loved it! You were just great. I never thought that rock and roll music would be such a turn on." She gave Keith a seductive smile and pose. After a few more minutes of hugging and kissing, he grabbed Connie's hand and led her to the bedroom and closed the door behind them. The other band members were busy in the parlor drinking, dancing, and partying with the other party goers.

In the room, Connie took her blouse off and started strutting for Keith. The singer reached into his overnight bag and pulled out a canister and a balloon. "What's that?" she wanted to know.

"It's a whippet." Having lived in a small town her entire life, Connie was a little naïve to the latest drug trends among teenagers. But she was willing to try it. He put the balloon over the seal and punctured the seal of the whippet canister. Gas began to fill the balloon.

"I want you to inhale some of this and hold your breath for as long as you can," he said. Connie took a big whiff of the gas in the balloon. Soon, she became light headed and dizzy. Then she started to hallucinate. Inanimate objects in the room started to move. Her body started to get numb.

"How does that feel" Keith said to her.

"I feel really good. I am so happy." But she was having some difficulty standing. Nevertheless, she said, "Can I have some more?"

"Here, take another hit." Connie took another big breath from the balloon and held her breath again.

After the second inhalation, the lights in the room began to spin around her brain. Connie collapsed onto the bed and was unconscious. Her face was turning blue.

"Hey, this is not what supposed to happen," he told her.

"Get up. Let's have some fun" Keith said. He tried to arouse her but it was no use. Keith ran out of the room and shouted for someone to call an ambulance. But when it arrived, it was too late. Connie was dead.

The police interviewed everyone at the party. Whippet canisters and balloons were confiscated as evidence. The medical examiner also came and took the body away. To his credit, Keith was in complete compliance with the police. He told them exactly what happened and said that there was no malicious intent. Nevertheless, he was read his Maranda rights and arrested. Groove posted bail. His band suspended all future appearances pending his trial. In the end, Keith was tried and convicted of involuntary manslaughter and he was sentenced to 10 years in prison. His music career and the band *Toxic Blend* were over in a short breath.

*

A few months after his conviction, we had a discussion about Connie's death and Keith's criminal case since it made national headline news.

"Is there a clinical laboratory test that we can do to confirm or deny the presence of nitrous oxide," one of my techs asked. This was the gas present in the whippet canisters and the cause of the girl's death. It wasn't relevant in Connie's case because Keith admitted to having given her a whippet and the evidence was clear.

"No, it has an extremely short half-life and is broken down into nitrites and nitrates, both of which are normally found in the body," I responded. The next question was more difficult to answer.

"Why do some individuals appear to be particularly sensitive to nitrous oxide while the majority of individuals suffer no ill effects?"

"It is likely a pharmacogenomics effect," I told my students. This is a field of science studying the effect of genetic variances on the disposition and toxicity of drugs and medications. Since I knew nothing about the specific pharmacogenomics of nitrous oxide, I asked one of my toxicology postdoctoral fellows, Dr. Pamela Hopkins, to do a literature search. A week later, Dr. Hopkins came back with a response to the group.

"Death by nitrous oxide is due to suffocation or lack of oxygen delivery to the brain. The genetic cause of why some people suffer these effects while most are immune is currently unknown. I did find out that prolonged exposure to nitrous oxide inactivates vitamin B12." Everyone in my group knew that dietary deficiency of vitamin B12 and folate causes a form of anemia characterized by an increase in the size of human red blood cells. "Children with a defect in an enzyme called "MTHFR" have neurologic complications following brief exposure to nitrous oxide. There have been no autopsy studies conducted to date to see if there is a higher prevalence of this mutation among those who have died."

As a sort of warning to my group of students who are at the right age for whippet abuse, I made the following comment. "It would appear that recreational use of nitrous oxide is akin to playing Russian roulette. Most of the time, the gun chamber is empty. But you are taking a chance when you use this substance that your body will not react to this gas in a favorable manner.

Poor Connie was one of those who got the bullet."

*

Nitrous oxide has been used as an anesthetic for dental procedures starting in 1844. It is also known as "laughing gas" because of its euphoric effect. In 1914, Robert Goddard filed a patent for the use of nitrous as a rocket fuel propellant. It works by producing heat upon decomposing to nitrogen and oxygen. Nitrous oxide is still used in dental procedures today. It is safe because a controlled amount of oxygen is also administered in addition to the anesthetic gas. Nitrous oxide is found in cans of whipped cream. It is also sold over the internet for cooking purposes, but the real intent is its effect on sexual arousal.

The major health effect of nitrous oxide is the replacement of this gas for oxygen in the brain. Purposeful restriction of oxygen to the brain produces a condition known for its euphoric effect, also known as "erotic asphyxiation." The deprivation of oxygen causes a temporary accumulation of carbon dioxide leading to a light-headedness and stimulation of the brain's pleasure center. There are reports of people who hang themselves with a cord or strangle their sex partner to the point of near death, in order to heighten sexual arousal. The actor David Carradine died due to erotic asphyxiation while in Thailand. Individuals who abuse whippets achieve these same sensations through chemical means, but thought to be safer than choking. Throughout history, there have been a number of individuals who have used nitrous oxide, presumably for this purpose, including soccer player Kyle Walker, actress Michelle Keegan, and even England's Prince Harry. The actress Demi Moore was reportedly hospitalized in 2012 after using a whippet. She suffered a seizure and lapsed into semi-consciousness.

According to the Substance Abuse and Mental Health Services Administration, over 12 million people have tried it. Nitrous oxide does not have the same negative reputation as other street drugs such as cocaine, methamphetamine, or heroin. Many believe it to be safe and legal. Nitrous oxide is not regulated by the Drug Enforcement Agency. However, the FDA has banned sale and distribution of the gas for the purpose of human consumption.

Bagel

******

Calvin met with his team of scientists and marketing staff on a Monday morning. "We are going into a new line of business" he said to his group. Cao and the rest of the group looked at each other without any idea where this was going. "We are going to make 'test-at-home' drug testing devices." Most of the staff was confused by this statement. They all knew Calvin's personal story, that he worked in a drug testing laboratory where they performed thousands of tests on urine each day on employees. This testing was not conducted for medical purposes. It was to determine if someone in the workforce was using a drug without proper medical supervision or authorization.

The first test was a combination of a "screening" test which determined if a particular class of drug was present. If someone uses morphine, the urine screening test would detect the presence of an "opiate," a general term that indicates a class of drugs. In addition to morphine, other drugs such as codeine, heroin, Vicodin, or Dilaudid are specific drugs that are part of the opiate family. A positive screening test would trigger the use of a second more definitive laboratory test on the same original urine sample. Mass spectrometry is an instrument used to identify the specific drug present and measure how much was present in the urine. If the concentration of morphine exceeds the cutoff concentration for the confirmatory assay, the result is reported to a "Medical Review Officer." The MRO's job is to determine if the lab test result was indicative of abuse by that drug, or if there were legitimate reasons for the drug to be present, such as a doctor's prescription.

"We've been missing the boat," Calvin said to his staff. "While all official workplace drug testing is conducted in certified laboratories, there is a big market for self-testing by consumers."

Cao was the first to assimilate the information that Calvin was stating. "I get it!" he said to the others. "Today, most testing is conducted for pre-employment purposes. If someone wants a job at many companies, the job applicant must pass a urine test before a final offer is issued. If we sold an over-the-counter drug test to someone who uses drugs, they could test their urine in the privacy of their homes before they subject themselves to the real test."

"Precisely," Calvin said. "Drugs stay in our bodies for 2-3 days. A person could abstain from using drugs and test themselves using our device before they donate a urine sample for the real test. If the result turns positive for a drug, they can reschedule the drug test for a later date. If the at-home test turns negative for all drugs tested, the person can keep the appointment. It's like having the answers to a written test ahead of time."

"That's great. After all cheating is our business," Cao concluded.

*

Sylvia Lawrence was a creature of habit. She worked at the school as a secretary. Each morning, she pulled up to the doughnut shop's drive through window and ordered a cup of coffee with cream and sugar, and a sesame seed bagel with cream cheese. She parked her car and walked into the employee lounge to have her breakfast. Sylvia lived with her mother who complained to her about this habit.

"You should take the time to eat a full breakfast, Sylvia. I will cook you whatever you want in the morning."

"No, Mom, school starts very early and I don't have time to eat breakfast at home. This is faster."

Sylvia kept to her routine for many years. Then one day, near the beginning of a new school year, her life took a dramatic turn. Terrance was one of the new gym teachers who came to the office one day looking for some blank attendance forms. When he saw Sylvia, he stopped in his tracks and was immediately attracted to her. It was a little awkward at first because he stood at the front of Sylvia's desk without saying anything. Finally Sylvia spoke. "Is there something I can do for you?"

"I'm looking for some attendance forms," he said. "You have the prettiest eyes."

Sylvia was attracted to Terrance as well. He was tall, muscular, and had an attractive smile. "They are just over here" she said as she reached for them without taking her eyes away from Terrance's face.

"My name is Terrance. I am one of the new gym teachers. What is your name?"

"Sylvia. It is nice to meet you," she said. She offered her hand and he shook it.

Terrance wasted no time. "Would you care to join me for lunch today? I don't have a fifth period class."

Sylvia hesitated for a brief moment. There was nothing in the school's regulation about dating colleagues. Many of the teachers were married to each other. "Sure" Sylvia said.

"I'll come back around noon," Terrance said.

Over the next few months, Terrance and Sylvia saw each other regularly. By the time the school year ended 8 months later, they were a couple. They began making plans for the summer. Only a few teachers stayed on during the break to teach summer school. Most of the administrative staff also took the summer off. Terrance and Sylvia went on an extended road trip across America. They visited many state and national parks, camping along the way. When they returned to school in September, Sylvia moved out of her mother's house and into Terrance's apartment. She was also two months pregnant.

*

Western General Hospital was a small community hospital of 150 beds. It served several surrounding towns in a rural area of Western Pennsylvania. The laboratory director was a pathologist by the name of Dr. Casey Reynolds. Western General was not big enough to have more than one pathologist. Dr. Reynolds was responsible for reviewing biopsies, performing autopsies, and directing the clinical laboratory. Dr. Stuart Fleming was the director of the emergency department at Western. One day, Dr. Fleming came to see Dr. Reynolds.

"We need to have toxicology tests available in the ED," he told the pathologist.

"But we rarely see drug overdoses in our community. It would be very expensive to set up a drug testing service for the occasional case that we see," Dr. Reynolds replied.

"It is true that drug abuse is infrequent in our community," Dr. Fleming agreed. "But when it occurs, we need some help in making a diagnosis. We cannot wait a day for results to return from the University Hospital. What can the lab do to help us while still being cost effective?"

"I'll get back to you," Dr. Reynolds said.

Over the course of the next few weeks, Dr. Reynolds consulted with Dottie, his senior laboratory technologist and investigated his options for performing drug testing in house.

"We do have the equipment in the laboratory to do testing but as you know, we have to perform calibration, quality control testing, and proficiency testing each night. This is a waste of money if we don't get any test requests," the senior tech said.

"What if we do these steps only on the days that we have a request for toxicology testing?" Dr. Reynolds asked.

"It takes our techs an hour or two to set up the instrument. In the meantime, they are not available for the other tests that are required. But there is another way," Dottie said.

With Dottie's help, Dr. Reynolds found out about products offered by Test-Me, Inc. These were over-the-counter toxicology testing devices that required little training and were very inexpensive. The laboratory contacted the company who sent out a few samples of their testing devices along with instructions. In later discussions with Dr. Fleming, there were three tests of particular interest, one for cocaine, another for methamphetamine, and the third one for opiates. After a brief study, Dottie went into Dr. Reynold's office.

"These are really easy to use. We compared our results against those obtained from the University Hospital. Our techs had no problem performing the tests and getting the right result. I will write up a procedure, train our second and third shift personnel, and purchase a supply of kits. We should be ready to offer this test in a month or so."

*

Now that they were roommates, Terrance and Sylvia drove to school together every day. Sylvia continued to stop at the doughnut shop in the morning. This school year, she changed from sesame seed bagels to ones containing poppy seeds. "Every girl needs a change once in a while," she told Terrance.

"Wow, what a big change. Will tomorrow be strawberry cream cheese?" Terrance teased her.

"Shut up and drive the car big boy."

Sylvia was very diligent during her pregnancy. She was compliant with all of her pre-natal appointments and recommendations. She was never a heavy drinker but she abstained from all alcohol while pregnant and under the care of her obstetrician, Dr. Harriet Compton. She also told Terrance that smoking was no longer permitted in their small apartment, so he went outside to light up. Terrance was a very willing participant. He took all of the birthing classes that were offered by the General. Sylvia maintained a moderate exercise program throughout her pregnancy. Her morning sickness was minimal, and she did not gain much weight. She told the school that she hoped to work right up to the day of her child's delivery.

Soon, that day came. It was the Friday before the Easter Holiday. During lunch, Sylvia started getting regular contractions. She called Terrance at the gym where he was teaching, and told him it was time. Upon getting word, he dismissed his class and ran to the office. He helped her into his car and they drove to Western General. Dr. Compton was away on a week-long vacation, but his partner was on call and performed the delivery. After a brief labor of only 4 hours, the cry of a newborn baby girl was heard in the maternity ward. They named her Rebecca. Sylvia was three weeks early in her delivery and the child weighed 5 pounds and 3 ounces. While Sylvia was discharged from the hospital after 48 hours, Rebecca stayed a few more days because of her prematurity. Sylvia and Terrance took Rebecca home on her fourth day of life.

A day later, Sylvia and Terrance were visited by a police officer and Louise Bertha from the State child welfare department.

"We need to see your child," the officer stated.

"What is this all about?" Terrance asked.

When Sylvia returned with the child, Louise spoke up. "Western Hospital has conducted a drug test on you and your child. You both came out positive for a metabolite of heroin. By the powers invested to me by the State of Pennsylvania, we are taking custody of your child following an investigation of you and your husband's suitability as parents. If we find that you are unfit, we will permanently remove your baby, and put her up for adoption. Officer, please remove the child from this home."

"What, you can't do this!" Sylvia exclaimed. "We have done nothing wrong. Terrance, please stop them!"

While the officer was taking the child he warned the father. "Do not interfere. You will have a chance to explain yourself. If you resist, I will have to take both of you to the county jail. Don't make this any more difficult than it is."

The baby was removed without any further explanation. Terrance contacted an attorney, John Corcorin, who was a family friend. He met with a hospital official regarding the nature of the child's removal.

*

Western General instituted a drug testing policy for all newborns who are classified as being "low birth weight," defined as an infant weighing less than 5 pounds 8 ounces at birth. This was a highly controversial decision made by the hospital.

"It is well known that women who abuse drugs during their pregnancy have a much higher frequency of delivering smaller babies than non-drug abusing mothers," Louise Bertha from the city's child welfare department explained.

"But there are dozens of reasons for a low birth weight baby," Dr. Compton said. "Aren't we violating the civil liberties of our patients by doing this?"

"We have to protect newborns during this most critical time of their life. If we don't, nobody else will. We must take a 'zero tolerance' stance against any hint of drug abuse by a mother while she is pregnant" Louise said.

"What about the rights of the mother?" Dr. Compton asked.

"We can ways return the child after we're sure there is no abuse. But if we keep the child with the mother, there could be irreversible harm" Louise was digging her heels into this debate. She had first-hand experience regarding newborn abuse by drug-addicted parents.

"There are certain behaviors that increase the likelihood of drug abuse. Couldn't we focus on these women and not test everyone who happens to deliver a small baby?" Dr. Compton pleaded.

"Such a policy is subjective and would be open for 'racial profiling.' We have to treat all patients equally under a well-defined and objective policy," Louise stated.

"I never said anything about profiling," Dr. Compton said. "I simply want to be reasonable about this."

*

John Corcorin met with hospital officials and Louise Bertha the next day to find out why Rebecca was removed from the family.

"Both the mother and daughter tested positive for heroin. It is in the child's best interest to be removed until we can conduct an investigation," Louise said.

*

I got the call from Pennsylvania because of a study one of my graduate students conducted some 10 years ago. The first thing I requested was to examine the laboratory data that surrounded the decision made by Western General and the Child Welfare Department. When I received the data, I confirmed that both the mother and child's urine sample that had been collected immediately after the infant's delivery were positive for morphine. But I quickly learned that the confirmatory mass spectrometry procedure was not performed.

"Mr. Corcoran, in the absence of the second more definitive test, the hospital cannot conclude that Sylvia was abusing heroin at the time. With this screening test result, the most they can say is that she was using some opiate product. There are many prescription and some over-the-counter analgesics that can produce this result. Is there a prescription record of medications that she took just before delivery? Was any drug given during labor?" I asked.

"She denies any drug use at any time during her

pregnancy. Medical records show that she was only given an epidural anesthetic during delivery. I am told by the lab that this doesn't trigger the positive urine drug test result," Corcoran concluded.

"That is correct. Anesthetics such as bupivacaine do not produce positive drug test results. Based on what you have told me, I think I know what happened to Sylvia and can I prove her innocence."

From what Corcoran told me about Sylvia's dietary habits, I explained my theory and gave instructions for Sylvia to follow. I then said to Corcoran, "If this plan is to work, it is very important that you don't tell her why we are asking her to do this. The child welfare committee must be convinced that nothing was contrived here." Corcoran agreed with my plan and Sylvia was called and asked to follow her lawyer's precise instructions. When all of the steps were completed, Sylvia produced a urine sample that was sent to my laboratory for analysis. There we performed a special analysis not offered anywhere else in the world.

It took my lab just one afternoon to obtain the result I was suspecting. I called John Corcoran and told him of my findings.

"The hearing on Sylvia's case is tomorrow. Can you fly in and testify on her behalf?" he asked.

"Definitely, we need to set this record straight." I booked a "red-eye" flight and was in Pittsburgh by the next morning. Someone from Corcoran's office met me at the airport and we drove directly to Western General for the hearing that afternoon. I was introduced to Sylvia and Terrance who thanked me for coming. Sylvia was noticeably trembling. Her eyes were blood-shot from prolonged crying. When the time came, I faced Louise Bertha and the other members of the child welfare committee. Sylvia and Terrance sat in the back holding hands.

"Under instructions by Mr. Corcoran, we had Sylvia retrace her steps the day before and day of her delivery," I told them. "She ate the same lunch at the school and dinner at home with Terrance. The next morning, she underwent the same daily routine, stopping by the doughnut shop, ordering coffee and a bagel. She had nothing more to eat that morning when she and Terrance drove to the hospital to deliver Rebecca. With Sylvia's prior consent, Mr. Corcoran asked a female member of his law firm to take Sylvia into the bathroom and witness Sylvia urinating into a cup. This sample was sent to my laboratory for analysis."

"What did you find, Doctor?" Louise inquired.

"We used the same drug testing device that was used here at Western General and found morphine in her urine sample. This test is not designed or is able to detect heroin," I stated. There was an audible murmur within the room. Sylvia started to cry again. She buried her face into Terrance's shoulder. *I do not use drugs. Why is this happening to me?*

"But Sylvia and Terrance have sworn that she has never taken any drugs of this kind. The positive morphine comes from eating a bagel each morning containing poppy seeds. This is the source of the opiates in her urine on the day of her child's delivery and the morning that we received her urine sample," I said to the panel.

Louise spoke up. "Doctor, that is a little too convenient, don't you think? Do you have any proof that these seeds actually contained morphine?"

I was prepared for this line of questioning. "It is true that not all poppy seeds contain opiates. It depends on how thoroughly the seeds are washed before they are used. We didn't tell Sylvia or Terrance or the doughnut shop what we were planning. Sylvia precisely retraced her steps from the morning of her baby's delivery. There was no way she could have manipulated the results. After Sylvia left, Mr. Corcoran's assistant and I went back to the shop and purchased bagels from the same batch. I instructed my lab techs to remove the seeds, and have them tested for the presence of morphine. We found that they were positive in sufficient quantities to trigger a positive opiate result in Sylvia's urine. We also have her credit card receipt showing that she was in the store on that morning."

The Committee huddled to one side to discuss these latest findings while we waited. A few minutes later, Louise asked another question that I had anticipated.

"Doctor, you just said that the amount of opiates found in the seeds is variable. How do we know that the seeds Sylvia ate THAT day contained any drugs?"

"I do have proof that the seeds Sylvia ate on that occasion did contain opiates. In addition to morphine and sometimes codeine, poppy seeds contain other opiate compounds that are not found in the pharmaceutical parathion of opiate drugs or in recreational heroin. My laboratory has shown that thebaine is present in poppy seeds and in the urine of individuals eating these seeds. Our studies have shown that thebaine is consistently absent in patients who use and abuse drugs. In controlled trials of volunteers eating poppy seeds, thebaine is consistently present. The laboratory here was very cooperative. They retained Sylvia's urine sample and allowed us to test a small portion for the presence of the naturally occurring compound. I have our reports here. Thebaine was in her urine sample both on the day of our re-creation of events, and on the day the sample was taken immediately following Rebecca's birth. There wasn't enough urine remaining after Rebecca's test, but we do know that drugs cross the placenta from mother to child. With Sylvia's permission, we even found thebaine in her breast milk."

Dr. Compton then got up and spoke on Sylvia's behalf. "I have records of Sylvia's pre-partum examinations. She was as compliant a patient as I ever have had. If she was a heroin addict I would know about it. Your investigators have found no evidence of drug use in their household. I demand that her child be returned to her immediately."

The Committee deliberated again for a few minutes and returned with their decision. "Based on the testimony presented today at this hearing, the Committee has agreed to return Rebecca to the custody of Sylvia and Terrance. This matter is closed."

No apologies were given by the Committee. With Dr. Compton by their side, Sylvia and Terrance rushed to the newborn ward to retrieve their baby. Tears were flowing down her face once again.

*

This story is based on the case of Elizabeth Mort whose 3-day old baby named Isabella was removed from her custody in April 2010. Like Sylvia, Elizabeth had eaten a bagel containing poppy seeds. The child was returned to her mother five days later. Three years later, the

American Civil Liberties Union of Pennsylvania filed a lawsuit on behalf of the mother, against Jameson Hospital where the child was born. The hospital and the child welfare agency settled the lawsuit for $143,500. As a result, Jameson Hospital changed their newborn toxicology testing policy.

A decision to remove a child from the custody of their parents requires a complete understanding of the current toxicology laboratory testing policies. Unfortunately, some individuals empowered with these decisions are not knowledgeable about testing limitations and do not take the time to contact the laboratory personnel to learn. As a result, mistakes like these have occurred.

At home testing devices are available for urine drug testing. These tests are not as robust as the ones used in the clinical laboratory. There can be errors in how the test is performed and interpreted. For the opiate test, there are also differences in the cutoff concentration used to report a positive result. Devices used in the hospital for clinical toxicology purposes such as at Jameson Hospital, have a low cutoff of 300 ng/mL. The Substance Abuse and Mental Health Administration who administers Federal Workplace drug testing established an opiate cutoff of 2000 ng/mL cutoff. This higher cutoff was set in order to reduce the incidence of positive test results due to poppy seed consumption. Urine drug tests used by hospital and family welfare committees to make decisions regarding custody should also use a 2000 ng/ml cutoff. Because the screening tests suffer from false positive test results, all urine drug tests conducted for forensic purposes must be confirmed by a definitive assay such as mass spectrometry. Failure to use this test can result in mistakes that can have significant consequences to donors of urine samples. The device made by Calvin's lab and used at Western General had the wrong opiate cutoff level for the intended purpose.

Flush

****

Calvin befriended many jocks during his time at the gym. Soon, he was going out to bars with his weight-lifting friends to have a brew after workouts. Most of these men took great pride in how their bodies looked to others. There are always plenty of mirrors in a weight-lifting gym. Each day, the gym staff inspects the mirrors and maintains them in spotless condition. Several of these body builders were gay. But this fact didn't bother Calvin. They knew he was straight and once had a wife and child. Over time, many of his gym buddies learned what Calvin did for a living. They didn't understand the drug masking and adulteration part of his company, but they certainly knew about the use of performance enhancing drugs. Soon they were asking him to supply them with growth hormone, anabolic steroids and other supplements. Calvin tried to keep his personal life away from his business concerns. But his two main interests in life were intertwined. The vast majority of the men who trained at this gym did so for physical fitness purposes only and did not enter into body building contests or aerobic competitions. One day, Calvin had a conversation with one of his gym friends about performance enhancing drugs or PEDs.

"I just want to look better for the ladies," Juan-Sebastian told Calvin one day after lifting. Juan-Sebastian was a good looking man but shorter than average. He liked tall women and believed that a better physique might work to his advantage. He was not a competitive athlete, so testing for the presence of performance enhancing drugs was not an issue for him.

"There may be some long-term health issues with prolonged use of PEDs," Calvin warned.

"I am not concerned about the distant future. I won't care when I am old and my mind is shot anyway. I am a believer of just today and now. Who knows, I could get hit by a semi-truck tomorrow. At least I will leave this world with a good looking body. Calvin, what can you do for me now?"

"There are several options," Calvin remarked. "You can take anabolic steroids, but this will lead to acne which could scar your body. We are making growth hormone now, which increases muscles by making more proteins. We have been selling it to athletes and actors. However, there have been reports of clinical depression with repeated use of this drug."

"I already have a history of depression in my family. My cousin committed suicide a few years back. I don't need to mess up my brain any more than it is already. Got anything else?" Juan-Sebastian asked.

"Gamma hydroxybutrate or GHB has been used by weight lifters for many years," Calvin told Juan-Sebastian. "GHB has been shown to naturally increase growth hormone in the body. At one time, it was used in a medical setting as a general anesthetic to treat clinical depression. It is approved today to treat narcolepsy, a sleep disorder. This might be just the thing for you."

"Do you sell this stuff"? Juan-Sebastian was very curious.

"No, it is really simple to make. All you need is gamma butyrolactone, which is a solvent used for stripping paint off furniture. Add a little alkali, heat it, and boom, GHB. I'll have the boys make some in the lab and I'll give you some at no charge. But if you use this, you have to stop drinking alcohol. This combination can cause a respiratory arrest."

"I don't drink much anyway," Juan-Sebastian said. "I'd be happy to abstain if this stuff works."

"And another thing," Calvin said. "If I give you this stuff, you must promise not to tell anyone else in the gym or at home that you're on it. I don't want to make GHB available to everyone. This is not why I come here each week. I don't need or want you guys as customers. I want to keep you as friends. You promise?"

"Swear to God and hope to die young," Juan Sebastian stated.

Within a few weeks, Juan-Sebastian was using GHB on a regular basis. Within a few weeks, Juan-Sebastian gained 25 pounds of muscle. He had more stamina and was able to work out harder. Some of Juan-Sebastian's friends noted the change in his physique and asked him about it. To Juan-Sebastian's credit, he never acknowledged taking any supplement and nobody knew that Calvin was supplying him with the drug. Juan-Sebastian did make one critical mistake. In his locker, he kept small amount of the drug in a glass vial labeled "GHB."

*

Kiko's family was originally from a small village in Japan. She and her parents moved to Southern California when she was 4 years old. They lived in an area of Los Angeles where there were many other Japanese families. Kiko did well in her studies and upon graduation from high school, she attended a neighboring junior college for the first two years. Then she transferred to UCLA where she earned a Bachelor's degree in Biology. During her four years of college, Kiko lived at home. When it was time to select a graduate school, she selected a pharmacology program in San Francisco. Kiko was 22 years old and was living away from her parent's home for the first time. It was in Northern California where Kiko transformed herself into a grownup woman. There was a degree of rebellion from having her freedom suppressed by her parents through all of her teenage years. Kiko bought more contemporary clothing, began wearing makeup, and started dating in groups for the first time. Within 6 months of her arrival, Kiko started going to nightclubs and dance clubs with her friends. She also started drinking alcohol. Kiko reacted very differently than her Caucasian friends when drinking. She didn't experience the usual euphoria of alcohol. Instead, she got sick and nauseated even after one drink. She also developed red flushes or blotches on her face, neck, and shoulders. But she really liked her friends and she felt pressured to drink in order to fit in. Over time, her body adjusted to alcohol and she was able to drink more.

Franklin was one of the graduate students in Kiko's class. He asked her out for dates on several occasions. Kiko was still new at "socializing" and she wasn't ready for a steady boyfriend.

"Let's just stay friends," she told him the third time he asked her out.

Being rejected made Franklin more determined than

ever to date Kiko. He started to go to the gym to work out and hope Kiko would notice. It was there that he met Juan-Sebastian.

"You have plenty of girlfriends," he told Juan-Sebastian. "How do you do it?"

"Women like men who behave naturally with them. Don't try to be someone you aren't. I have learned you can't force relationships."

That might work for you, Franklin thought. *You have that great tanned Latino look. I have pukey white skin with man-boobs. How can I get a girl? I need help.*

Soon Franklin found something that he thought was the answer to his problem. After a workout, Juan-Sebastian went to take a shower and accidently left his locker unlocked. With nobody looking, Franklin saw the GHB vial on the top shelf. That evening, Franklin did an internet search and learned that GHB was a body building supplement. He also learned that GHB can cause someone to become unconscious and suffer a temporary memory loss. The next time Juan-Sebastian left his locker unattended, Franklin opened the vial and stole a small amount of the GHB drug without anyone watching him. *He'll never know I took some. Let's see how good this stuff works* he thought.

*

That weekend, Kiko and a group of her friends including Franklin went to a party at a fraternity house. There was plenty of music, food, and drink. Kiko was having a good time and had her share of drinks. She was dancing with Franklin to the music. *Maybe this is my night with Kiko,* so Franklin encouraged her to drink more.

"Let me get you a beer from the keg," he said to her.

Franklin returned and she drank the beverage while dancing to the next tune. As the night went on, she became dizzy and disoriented. *I'm just going to lie down and take a nap*, she thought to herself. Kiko dropped down onto a couch and fell fast asleep. She was wearing spiked high heels at the time. The party went on for a few more hours before everyone had either left or passed out onto the furniture or floor.

The next morning, Kiko woke up with a severe headache. She was alone in a bed in a room at the fraternity. Her face was flushed red. She knew she had too much to drink last night. *I am never going to do this again* she vowed to herself. Kiko got up and went to the bathroom. A pain shot through her ureter when she started to urinate. She looked down and noticed a small amount of blood. Her labia also ached. Kiko knew the blood was not from her period, that had ended just a few days ago and it was too soon for the next one. Kiko got up and looked at herself in the mirror. She looked terrible. Her eyes were baggy and her makeup was runny. She then felt something digging into her back. She took her top off and turned her back to the mirror. Only one of the three hooks of her bra strap was connected to the clasp. The back strap containing the hooks was also twisted one complete revolution and then fastened to the other side. *I know I put the bra on correctly last night. What is going on here? I don't remember taking my clothes off. Somebody has unclipped and re-clipped my bra!* Kiko left the bathroom and wanted to leave. She was barefoot and went into the living room to look for her shoes. The room was a mess. There were a lot of beer cans, wine classes, plastic cups, plates, and uneaten snacks strewn about the room. Beneath the couch she found her shoes. She held them in her hands and walked barefoot to her apartment. Her head was still aching.

When she arrived home, Kiko told her roommate Sharon about last night. "There was some pain in my private areas when I woke up this morning."

"I was worried about you. It is unlike you to stay out all night. Where were you?" Sharon asked.

"I went to the sigma house down the street. I had too much to drink. I just rested my head on the couch to take a nap. Next thing I know, I woke up in a strange room. Do you think anything happened?" Kiko asked. "Also, I think my clothes have been rearranged."

"You need to go to the hospital and be checked out. You may have been date raped," Sharon said.

"But I wasn't with anybody. We went to the party as a group."

"It doesn't matter. Somebody may have spiked your drink and assaulted you when you were unconscious."

"That's disgusting!" Kiko said. "Who would do something like that? Wait, Franklin has been hitting on me for the past month. Do you think he is capable of this?"

"I'm taking you to the hospital right now to be examined," Sharon said. "Don't change your clothes. They may want to examine your clothing."

"I want to shower before going. I feel so dirty," Kiko said.

"Don't do that. You might remove any important evidence. Let's just go."

*

At the General, we have a standard procedure for investigating rape cases. A gynecologist is on staff to perform a thorough pelvic exam. An ER psychiatrist is also available for counseling. Kiko was brought in by Sharon and they were met by a triaging nurse. "I think my friend may have been raped last night."

Kiko was taken into a private room. Sharon was allowed to remain with her. Kiko removed all of her clothes which were placed into a paper bag. She was given a clean hospital gown to wear. She sat in the room waiting for the gynecologist to arrive. Dr. Francine Davis was experienced in examining women who had been raped. With Kiko's permission, Dr. Davis conducted an examination. With a speculum, she carefully examined Kiko for the presence of semen. She took a Q-tip and swabbed the inner walls of her vagina and put the swab into a tube. She then examined her vagina and vulvar areas for signs of forced entry. There was some redness around her labia but it was unclear if this was due to recent sexual intercourse. Kiko was questioned about her intercourse history. While she was not a virgin, she rarely had sex and reported no intercourse for the past 3 months. Blood and urine were also collected from Kiko.

A call was placed to my laboratory. I personally came down to the emergency department to take custody of the samples. If Kiko was raped and the perpetrator identified, I may have to go to court to testify on behalf of our patient. It is not a pleasant part of my job but often necessary. Fortunately, drug-facilitated date rape doesn't happen that often. Back in the clinical laboratory, we examined the swab for the presence of prostate specific antigen or PSA. This is a test we conduct in the laboratory for men who have prostate cancer. PSA is present in high concentration in seminal fluid but is absent in vaginal fluid unless there is recent intercourse. The sample was negative for the presence of PSA. However, this does not exclude the possibility of rape. Some attackers are either impotent or have undergone a vasectomy. Other attackers wear condoms or withdraw prior to ejaculation.

The blood and urine samples were tested for the presence of "date rape drugs." There are many drugs that can be used to incapacitate an individual for the purpose of a sexual assault. Alcohol is the oldest of these drugs. It is ideal because victims usually consume drinks willingly and to the point where they lose their inhibitions, judgement, or both. Sexual intercourse with an unconscious victim is rape in most jurisdictions. Dr. Davis noticed that Kiko had red blotches over her body. The doctor knew this as the "Asian flush" reaction. This would limit the amount of alcohol that Kiko could consume without getting sick.

"Kiko: How much alcohol did you drink last night?" Dr. Davis asked.

"I remember a couple of drinks but I don't tolerate alcohol very well. I know I was very tired last night and sat down on the couch. Next thing I remember is waking up in a strange bed."

Dr. Davis replied. "The lab reported that your blood is currently negative for alcohol. This confirms that you didn't have a lot to drink last night. The toxicology lab tested your urine for date rape drugs including flunitrazepam or Rohypnol, ketamine, zolpidem, and GHB. All of them were negative. Despite these negative findings, I believe you were assaulted last night while you were unconscious."

Kiko put her head on Sharon's shoulder and started crying. *Who could have done this to me?* She gathered herself and then asked the doctor an important question.

"Could I get pregnant from this?"

"We did a pregnancy test on your urine" Dr. Davis said. "You are not pregnant now, but the test does not turn positive for a few days after intercourse. The good news is that we didn't find any semen in your body. Nevertheless, we will have to do another pregnancy test in a few days."

Kiko started crying again. "What am I going to tell my parents?"

"That's completely up to you. You are an adult and you can make your own choices. Don't think about it now, go home and get some rest. I will report this to your school and they will send a counselor to speak with you later in the week." Dr. Davis had been through this process too many times before.

"In the meantime, we are going to send your clothing to the crime lab to see if there is any evidence of semen. Here is my business card. Call me any time if you think I can help." Kiko thanked the doctor and she left the room.

Kiko's clothing was taken to the laboratory where it was examined for the presence of seminal fluid where they found trace amounts. This confirmed that some sexual activity had occurred, mostly likely the previous night. Molecular analysis was conducted to determine the identity of the donor. The results were reported to the University Police Department for their investigation of the assault.

The police questioned everyone they could find who was at the party including all of the fraternity members and Kiko's friends and classmates. Most of them could not remember even seeing Kiko at the party. The investigators told some of the students that seminal fluid was found on the clothing and that they were working on getting a court order to obtain DNA from everyone present at the party. Many of the men contacted their family lawyers to determine the constitutionality of this action. When Franklin heard of this news, he went to the police station and told them that he had sex with Kiko that night in question. He had not seen or spoken to Kiko since then and he did not know of her accusations of rape. He claimed that Kiko consented to sex. The investigators individually interviewed Franklin, Kiko, and other students who remembered them at the party. Many of the party goers saw them dancing together and walking up to the bedroom where the sex took place. They described Kiko as being groggy but conscious and apparently willing. Kiko admitted dancing with Franklin but she did not remember consenting to sex. The detectives could not prove beyond a reasonable doubt that a rape had occurred, and no charges were filed against Franklin. Satisfied with this conclusion, the University did nothing further to investigate the accusations made by the victim. The University did file a report of this attack as required under the Jeanne Cleary Act for statistical reporting of a potential crime occurring on their campus. Kiko dropped out of school and returned to her family in L.A.

*

Alcohol is metabolized in the body through alcohol dehydrogenase (ADH), a liver enzyme that breaks alcohol down to acetaldehyde. This intermediate is further metabolized through aldehyde dehydrogenase (ALDH) to form acetate which is further broken down in the liver. There are genetic variances in the genes that encode these enzymes. Individuals of Asian descent can produce a variant ADH enzyme that breaks down alcohol at a much faster rate than normal. Some of these same individuals have an ALDH variant that reduces the breakdown of acetaldehyde. The end result is an accumulation of acetaldehyde. This intermediate metabolite is responsible for the "Asian Flush" reaction, a reddish coloration of the face, neck, and shoulders. Excess acetaldehyde is toxic to humans and can cause flushing, nausea, headache, confusion, vomiting, and light headedness. Some alcoholics are treated with disulfiram which inhibits ADH activity. When alcohol is consumed, there is an accumulation of acetaldehyde that produces these undesirable symptoms thereby producing a deterrent to further drinking.

Title IX was an amendment passed on June 23, 1972, it prohibited discrimination based on an individual's gender. One area of application was to ensure equal opportunity for men and women to participate in sports. Prior to this amendment, colleges and universities discriminated against women by supporting more sports for men. On April 4, 2011, Vice President Joe Biden stated that Title IX also refers to responsibilities that schools have in investigating sexual violence. When institutions become aware of possible sexual violence or harassment, they have an obligation to investigate the complaint beyond the criminal investigation. In order to meet Title IX obligations, the standard is the "preponderance of evidence," a lower bar of proof than "beyond a reasonable doubt" that exists for police investigations. Institutions also have a 60 day time limit to conclude their investigation, even if the criminal investigation is still pending. Kiko's university failed in their responsibilities under Title IX since they did not separately investigate the victim's accusation. The U.S. Education Department's Office of Civil Rights can investigate violations of Title IX regulations. Schools found in non-compliance can be subject to revocation of funding and other federal sanctions. Despite this amendment, many accusations of sexual assault at college campuses today are not investigated.

The administration of a date rape drug incapacitates the victim, rendering them vulnerable to a drug facilitated sexual assault. Both men and women have been victims of date rape. Alcohol has been used as a date rape drug for centuries. Other date rape drugs include flunitrazepam, a sedative, ketamine, an anesthetic agent used in the veterinary industry, zopidem, used as a sleep aid, and GHB. Except for flunitrazepam, each of these other drugs has a short half-life in blood. GHB has the shortest ranging from 15 to 60 minutes and is undetectable in blood after 12 hours. Franklin spiked one of Kiko's drinks with GHB. She was taken to the bedroom before she fell completely unconscious. Thereafter, she was raped by Franklin who used a condom. Some of his semen spilled onto her panties when it was removed after intercourse. It is difficult to prove date rape by GHB because blood and urine must be within a few hours after adulteration. This is usually impossible because the victim is usually asleep during this time. This case serves as advice to date rape victims. Evidence is needed to convict the perpetuator. Victims should seek medical attention immediately after an assault so that the laboratory can look for the presence of any date rape drugs before they are cleared from the body.

The pressure of peers is a driving force for young adults. It can alter an individual's logic and sense of what is right. Kiko knew that she was genetically predisposed to the effects of alcohol. Yet she continued to imbibe despite her own best health interests. Her early family life was such that she was not exposed to the temptations of youth. When she came of age, she went overboard trying to experience what she thought she was missing. Fortunately for her, she survived this experience and became stronger because of it.

The Beta Blocker Assassin

****

Sergei Bezukladnik never knew his father. He served in the
Russian army and was killed in a training accident before Sergei
was born. Distraught at her husband's death, Sergei's mother
became an alcoholic and she died before Sergei was 7. As he had
no relatives, Sergei was sent to an orphanage in the northern
region of the Soviet Union, just before the country's dissolution
into separate states in 1991. It was a cold dark place, where food
and love were scarce. The boys were not closely supervised so
there were many fights. Sergei was one of the smaller and
younger of the children boarded there, but he grew up to be
tough. Sergei left the orphanage at 18 and enlisted into the
army. There his aggressiveness and fighting skills which he
developed as a child were further honed by his sergeants. Sergei
was a very quiet cadet and he kept to himself. His superiors saw
something in the young man. After the completion of basic
training, he was offered a position within the Russian Intelligence
Agency. There, he received an additional 3 years of training. He
showed a particularly strong attribute in sharp shooting. He had
perfect vision, a low heart rate, and a steady hand. They taught
him about weapons, especially high powered rifles. They
groomed him to be an assassin. This suited him because he did
not like people and he had no friends. He detested alcohol

because this is how his mother died.

Upon completion of the program, Sergei was given a new identity, and sent to live in a neighboring state. He became Tomas Orlov because Sergei Bezukladnik was hard to pronounce even among Russians, difficult to spell and impossible to remember. All traces of Sergei Bezukladnik were expunged by the Agency, and Tomas Orlov's personal history was fabricated. The fictitious Tomas grew up on the outskirts of Moscow to cattle farmers. His parents were older and died of natural causes. Tomas had no brothers or sisters. That part did not require him to lie. Tomas assimilated into a normal life while hiding his true identity as a spy, while waiting for orders.

Tomas became a field service engineer for a telecommunications company. His job was to upgrade and repair damaged receivers. Each day, he received work orders through an internet portal and rarely had to speak to anyone. This occupation suited him very well. He went about his business each day and his progress was monitored by the success of his repairs as determined remotely by the spy agency. He preferred outdoor work rather than being cooped up in an office. This also minimized his contact with people. Sergei lived in a modest apartment on the outskirts of the city. For recreation, he hiked and would often go into the nearby mountains alone for target practices. He didn't shoot animals, but he wanted to keep his shooting skills sharp for when it was needed. In the winter, he regularly went cross country skiing. Over the years, he became very good at the sport. He would ski many miles over a weekend.

Tomas had a contact within the Agency by the name of

Dominika, who was in the field for over 10 years. They would meet in discreet places and discuss the needs of his assignments. Most of the time, Tomas was asked to do surveillance of politicians and important businessmen. His uniform, badge, and credentials enabled him to move in and out of public buildings. Tomas was also a master of disguise and he could change his appearance as needed for the job. Most of the tasks were uninteresting and tedious. He knew that the Agency was testing him for bigger and better things. Dominika gave Tomas access to the Agency's own firing range, and Tomas went there on a regular basis. Beside the rifle range's caretaker, Tomas was the only other person there at any given time.

After two years of mundane jobs, Dominika finally told Tomas of a very important assignment.

"Do you know Alexander Yelagin?" she asked Tomas.

"Yelagin of Yelagin Properties. He is the owner of several casinos and ski resorts," Tomas said.

"He is linked to the Russian mob and he is a key financial supporter of the progressive party. We believe that if key members of this party become elected, there will be significant changes in domestic policy. For example, they may change the leadership and focus of our Agency. Apparently, they have their own spy organization that they use for their own agenda. If Yelagin was eliminated, the money flow would stop. His sons have said in public that they do not support their father's political views."

Tomas sat in silence contemplating the task at hand.

"But you have to make it look like an accident. We don't want to create a martyr among the party members. If he were to all of a sudden turn up dead, there would be suspicion that could lead to more support, not less. So I want you to come up with an assassination plan. I have asked another one of our agents to come up with a plan as well. We will choose the one we like best. Leave now. I will contact you again in 4 to 6 weeks."

Tomas returned to his apartment, turned on his computer, and spent the next several days researching his target. Yelagin's wealth and businesses were inherited from his father. When Alexander was young, he was a competitive downhill skier and competed in many European racing events. That all ended when he crashed during a race and suffered a severe head injury. A video of this crash was well documented on You-Tube. Alexander caught the edge of a ski and went flying into the air. His body flipped backwards while traveling at speeds exceeding 100 kilometers per hour. He landed on his head and skidded down the hard and icy slope for another 200 yards. Although he was wearing a helmet, he suffered a severe concussion and he was unconscious at the scene. Paramedics loaded him onto a safety sled and he was sent to the hospital. Alexander suffered a fractured skull and remained hospitalized for the next two months. After 6 months of recovery, Alexander returned to work devoted his time to the family business, eventually becoming the owner when his father retired.

Yelagin maintained an interest in competitive skiing by sponsoring young talent and attending European races. It wasn't long before his interest expanded to cross-country racing events as well. One of the more popular events that Yelagin sponsored was biathlon. This is a winter sport that combines cross-country skiing and rifle shooting. The sport was first popular among

Norwegians as an alternative for military training. Since Tomas was accomplished in both skiing and sharpshooting, he came up with a plan whereby he could get close to Yelagin and into a situation where Yelagin was comfortable and unsuspecting.

Tomas pitched his plan to Dominika at a meeting the following month. He told her of an event that Yelagin sponsors each year so he was sure to be prominently present. Tomas would participate in the race. Then, during the shooting phase, there would be a planned accident. She thought the plan was plausible but she had some serious reservations.

"Have you ever been in a biathlon before?" she asked.

"No, but I am as fit as any biathlete and know I can compete with them," Tomas said. "We have a few months to go. There are some local qualifying events coming up. If I can make Yelagin's event, we can plan an attack there.

"You will need a partner as a diversion. I'll discuss this plan with the Agency. We'll get back to you."

A few days later, Tomas got word from Dominika that his plan was selected by the Agency among the two that were proposed. In preparation for the race, Tomas joined a local cross-country skiing club where both men and women trained for the biathlon. Through the club, Tomas purchased several 0.22 gauge Long Rifles that were standard equipment for the competition. He also purchased the latest ski equipment and clothing. Tomas had no trouble with posting a competitive time on the 20 kilometer cross-country track. And when he wasn't breathing hard, it was also easy for him to hit the 20 targets with his rifle. But he soon learned why this event is so difficult. The competition requires accurate shooting in between vigorous laps on the cross-country race track. One minute is added to the cross-country ski race time for each missed target.

Even though Tomas was in great physical shape, his heart and respiration raced to a high rate, which greatly affected the accuracy of his shooting. He needed a means to lower his blood pressure and pulse rate so that he could be more accurate. Tomas read that during the 2008 Summer Olympics in Beijing, King Jong-su, a Korean athlete, was stripped of his silver metal after he won in the 10 meter and 50 meter pistol event. After the race, his urine was collected which tested positive for propranolol, a widely used beta blocker drug used in clinical practice. Propranolol is a drug used to treat patients after they have suffered a heart attack or if they have heart failure. It regulates the heart to maintain a slow regular rhythm. Tomas asked Dominika to obtain a supply of these drugs for his use in the biathlon. Tomas knew that no drug testing was going to be conducted during these local events. The assassin began training with the drug and learned how to shoot his rifle in between heart beats. His accuracy improved dramatically to the extent that he now posted times that qualified him for the event sponsored by Yelagin Properties.

*

A half a world away, another man had a conversation with a woman about the same drug at nearly the same time.

"Mom, you need to take metoprolol in addition to all of your other medications each day to control your heart rhythm," I said to her. At 85 years old, she was a week past her second successful surgery to replace her cardiac mitral valve.

"I'll sort these new pills and put one for each day into

my daily pill organizer" she said. My mother was an ideal patient. She was always compliant with her medications. "Should we do blood measurements for metoprolol levels," she asked me.

"No, this is not something we do in my clinical laboratory nor is needed in clinical practice," I responded. "You will be able to resume your normal activities. But don't think you can do a double flip off the uneven parallel bars." She had no idea what that meant but knew that it was a joke so she ignored it like so many of my other jokes.

*

Tomas met with Dominika and showed her that he was invited to participate in the event. The diversion plan would be Dominika's responsibility. "Based on the previous year's events, we know that Yelagin will be positioned near the finish line in a box constructed for his group. These seats are also adjacent to the targets so that Yelagin can see how well each competitor does in the shooting phase of the event," Dominika said. "You need to make sure that your aim is perfect. You won't have a second chance."

"Don't worry, his head is much bigger than the usual target." In biathlon, the target diameter is 1.8 inches when the shooter is in the prone position and 4.5 inches when the shooter is in the standing position.

There were thirty-five competitors for the event. The event was held on a chilly Saturday afternoon, but there was no wind or precipitation. Several hundred spectators and family members were in attendance both seated in the stands around the course. As expected, Yelagin and his entourage were in their special box. Dominika was a few rows further up, watching the proceedings alone. Tomas was given a bib that contained his competition number. He put it on over his ski suit. The announcer called each competitor to the starting line. With a shot from the starting gun, the race began. There were 5 laps of a 4 kilometer track. At the end of the first and third laps, racers shot at targets from the prone position. After the second and fourth laps, they shot from the standing position. The race would end after the fifth lap. The competitor with the best times including the penalty minutes added for any missed targets would be the winner.

Tomas was near the middle of the pack at first. His rifle was in a sling on his back. His plan was to shoot Yelagin after the second lap while standing. He didn't want to wait until the end of the race for fear of being tired. The race began simultaneously for all of the competitors. Later in the race, Tomas stayed near the back of the pack. His objective was not to distinguish himself by being a front runner, nor tire himself out to the point where he loses shooting accuracy. He also needed to have some separation between himself and any of other competitors so that the diversion plan would work. When he rounded the second lap, he positioned himself in the first bin closest to the stand.

Just as he removed the rifle from its sling, a woman jumped out of the stand and started running towards the shooters. She was shouting "Stop! Stop! You're hurting me." The woman was obviously delusional as there was nobody near her to cause her harm. It was part of Dominika's careful plan to cause a significant disruption to the race. She ran straight up toward Tomas as he was preparing to take his first shot. She got to him before race officials knew what was happening. Tomas pretended that he didn't see her or know what was going on. But according to their scheme, she bumped Tomas's arm that was holding the gun. As she did, the rifle swung up and toward the crowd that was seated immediately above the target area. At that precise moment, just as they had practiced, he pulled the trigger, and the bullet fired. In the following moments, there was significant chaos. Spectators ran to take cover after hearing a rifle shot. It wasn't clear at first if anyone was hurt. Members of Yelagin's entourage looked at their boss and one of them pushed his employer to the ground, away from the shooter in case there were more shots. Yelagin was not hit. Tomas had apparently missed his mark.

Race officials stopped the event and immediately went toward all of the competitors to confiscate their weapons. It was not clear if this was a planned event or simply an accident. When all of the commotion died down there was a woman who was lying on her back near the last row of stands. There was a bullet hole in her forehead. Another woman from the row below her saw the slain woman and screamed. Nobody knew who the victim was. She had no identification with her and she had come to the event alone. But Tomas knew who she was. It was Dominika. This was no accident. Tomas *was* successful in hitting his target.

Police were called and Tomas and the woman who created the diversion were taken into custody. They were questioned and held. An investigation proceeded to determine if there was a conspiracy to commit murder or if this had been an accident. Over the ensuing weeks, there was no connection found between the woman who created the diversion. She had

had a history of psychiatric illnesses although it was fabricated by Russian Intelligence. Tomas was in good standing with his employer. A further investigation showed that Dominika was a frequent visitor to Yelagin's casino and she had incurred a significant amount of debt. The authorities were unable to connect Dominika's death to Tomas and he was released.

Tomas found out about Dominika's motives to kill Yelagin a few days before the race. At that point, he wasn't going to risk killing a well-known figure in the community for Dominika's own personal purposes. But he didn't want Dominika to blow his cover either, so he decided to kill her instead of Yelagin. Knowing that she was not acting on orders from the Agency, he wasn't worried that the Agency would make a move against him. A few weeks after the shooting, Tomas left town without telling his boss. He also retired from the Agency. Due to the shroud surrounding this race, Tomas was banned from any further biathlon events.

*

The beta blocker pharmacology industry in the U.S. has been estimated to be around $2 billion. In addition to propranolol, metoprolol and atenolol are the ones most commonly prescribed for patients with cardiac disease. These drugs work by blocking the uptake of neurotransmitters at the synapse of nerves. This causes dilation of blood vessels and decreased blood pressure. Some individuals suffer side effects from taking beta blockers, including fatigue, headache, upset stomach, constipation, and diarrhea. Overdose concentrations can lead to seizures and death.

Recently, Dr. Joseph Mercola, a doctor who publishes a regular health newsletter has stated that based on a medical report, some 800,000 Europeans have died using beta blockers over a five-year time span. Many cardiologists and doctors who follow national and international clinical practice guidelines would disagree with Dr. Mercola's contention.

The World Anti-Doping Agency lists cardiac drugs including beta-blockers among the substances banned for use by athletes. There are many sports where such drugs improve athletic performance. In addition to biathlon and pistol shooting, beta blocker abuse also occurs among archers, curlers, and gymnasts. The Professional Golf Association has banned beta blocker drug use in 2008.

The anti-anxiety properties of these drugs also make them an attractive performance enhancer. Some musicians, singers, dancers, and actors who have stage fright have abused beta blockers in advance of giving performances in order to improve their shows. Students taking standardized exams have also used beta-blockers as a means to increase test scores. In one study of high school students who retook the SAT test, their score improved by 130 points. Typically, only a 30-point improvement is observed with re-testing.

A .22 gauge rifle does not inflect the same degree of injury as high powered guns that were used in the early days of the biathlon competition, and victims of these shots can survive. Up until 1965, powerful 0.30-06 Springfield and 7.62x51 mm NATO rifle cartridges were used in biathlon races. Guns using these bullets were used for sniper fire.

Skater

****

Calvin took several weeks off to visit Moscow. He had never been to an Eastern European country before, so his visit was remarkable. He did the usual things, visited the Kremlin, saw a ballet at the Bolshoi Theater, and even took a boat ride at Gorky Park. After a few days, he got bored and wanted to do something that might help his business. *If I find something, I can write my trip off as a business expense,* he thought. *My accountant will be very happy.* He learned about a pharmaceutical company that was producing a novel drug that had anti-ischemic properties. Use of this drug increases blood flow by dilating blood vessels to the heart and brain so that users experience improved physical and mental endurance. Calvin's interest was especially piqued when he learned that the drug was not cleared by the FDA for use in the U.S., and is not listed by the U.S. Drug Enforcement Agency as a "Scheduled" drug. *Hmm, maybe there is an opportunity for Test Me,* Calvin thought.

When Calvin returned home, he scheduled a meeting of his executive group the next morning. They all thought he was going to show pictures of his visit. Cao wasn't interested in sightseeing photos so he stayed in the lab. When they all assembled and Calvin noticed his chief scientist's absence, he asked about Cao's whereabouts.

"He is in the lab because he didn't want to see your

collection of matryshka dolls," one of Cao's lab techs said. "We came because we were hoping we'd all get a set."

"That's not why I called you here. Somebody call Cao to attend, please," the boss said. The call was placed and within a few minutes, Cao arrived.

"What did you want to show us, boss," Cao said somewhat impatiently. Instead of travel pictures, Calvin showed a chemical structure onto the screen.

"Anybody know what this is?" the boss wanted to know.

Cao responded. "Let's see, it has a carboxylated trimethylhydrazinium functional group, attached to a propanoate group, perhaps an isomer of butyrobetaine...."

Calvin raised his hand to stop his scientist from rambling on any further. "I'm sorry I asked. This is meldonium. It is an anti-ischemic drug. I found out that some of the Russian athletes are using this to increase their performance. It is not a banned substance by any of the Olympic or International athletic governing bodies."

"What is the medical evidence that it works?" Cao asked.

"There is none really. But it doesn't matter. If athletes think they can gain an edge, they will us it. Especially if it is not banned and nobody in the U.S. is testing for it. I want this to be our next product.

Cao confirmed that indeed meldonium was analogue of gamma-butyrobetaine, a chemical constituent normally found in the human body. This compound is converted to carnitine, an amino acid derivative that is involved in the conversion of fat into energy. Once Cao obtained the starting ingredients, it was a rather simple matter of hydroxylating it to meldonium. Within a month, Test Me had a new product. Calvin called it "Melba." It was a pleasing sounding name and reminds people of melba toast.

*

Maartje was born in Amsterdam. Both of her parents were highly athletic. Her mother played soccer in college and her father, Etienne, was a speed skater. He competed in the Elfstedentocht, which was last held in 1997. This is a 120-mile long speed skating competition that takes place along the frozen canals, rivers and lakes of Holland's Friesland Province. In recent years, the Dutch winters have not been cold enough to fulfil the requirement that the ice be at least 15 cm thick along the entire course. That year, the Netherlands experienced an extended cold spell and the race was held. Maartje's father finished in the top 50 of the 300 registered contestants. There were thousands of other skaters who participated in a concurrent leisure tour. A few years later, Etienne retired for competitive skating, and soon thereafter, he and his family immigrated to Wisconsin. Maartje was 10 years old at the time.

Maartje continued the skating tradition by joining a skating club once they moved to Madison. This was one of the premiere centers for speed skating with many former and current Olympians. Her father was her coach during the first few years of competition at the junior level. By the time she was ready for open adult competition, she hired a full time coach. Etienne was highly involved and stayed on as an advisor. While Etienne's best events was long distance skating, Maartje excelled in the sprints. She was invited to the Olympic trials at the age of 16. It was her first chance to go to the Olympics. Her father never made the Dutch National team having tried three times. Even though

Holland is much smaller in population than the U.S., speed skating is sort of their national sport and the competition, especially among males, was fiercer than in America.

The Winter Olympic Games have 5 distances for long track speed skating. Based on her times, Maartje qualified for the women's 500 and 1000 meters events and signed up for the US Olympic Team speed skating trials. The trial took place over 4 days. The 1000 meters was on the second day and the 500 meters on the third day of the trials. Maartjie and her father arrived to the Salt Lake City Utah venue two days early in order to get her acclimated to the altitude, rink and its environment. During the practice runs, she was extremely nervous and was visibly shaking. Her father tried to calm her down.

"Imagine that we're back in Holland and you and I are leisurely skating at our pond," he said to her. "You can handle this, there is nothing to be concerned about." Her father's words helped a little, but her body continued to tremble. Etienne went to see one of the trainers from the US National Team for an examination.

"Does your daughter have a history of seizures?" he asked.

"No, not that I know of," Etienne said.

"Perhaps her shaking are partial seizures. I am going to give her a medication that could help," the trainer said. "When you get home, she needs to see a neurologist."

"This is not going to get her into any trouble with the US Antidoping Agency, right?" Etienne asked. The USADA ensures that athletes who participate in international sporting events are free from any performance enhancing drugs and chemicals.

"Don't worry, this drug is not on the USADA banned list," he said.

With that, he gave Maartje meldonium that he purchased from Test Me, LLC. The drug seemed to calm her nerves and stopped her tremors. She competed exceptionally well and turned in PBs or "personal bests" in both events. While these times were not enough for her to win a spot on the team, she and her father were encouraged by her performance.

"If we continue to train for the next four years, I am sure you will make the team then," her father said. Before they left the arena, Etienne asked the trainer as to where he could purchase "Melba." The trainer gave Etienne the web address of Test Me, LLC.

Over the course of the next four years, Maartje continued to train hard for the next US Olympic Trials. Each year, her times improved. She won the gold medal in the 500 meter and silver in the 1000 meter in last year's World Games and was the favorite to win gold in this Olympic year. Etienne continued to purchase Melba for her daughter's daily use. About three months before the Olympic Trials, Maartje received a letter from the World Anti-Doping Agency.

"Effective this September, WADA will be testing urine of all current and potential Summer and Winter Olympic athletes for the presence of meldonium, a drug used to treat heart disease. We have determined that meldonium provides athletes increased exercise capacity and gives an unfair performance advantage to users. If you are using this drug for medical purposes and you produce a positive urine drug test result, you must provide a physician's prescription to WADA. Beginning January of next year, meldonium will be banned from all athletes irrespective of their medical condition. This grace period is to allow users of meldonium to alter their therapeutic regimen."

Maartje contacted her father and told him about the letter she received. "Is the medication that I am on?" she asked. This news was devastating to her father.

"Yes, you have been on this drug for the past three and one half years," Etienne said to his daughter. There was a pause, then he said, "I can't believe they are banning this now, with the Olympic trials just around the corner. How can they do this to us? We need to fight this. Let me see the letter."

"Dad, relax. I am older and more experienced now. I don't think I need this drug to control my shaking. I will just stop taking it," Maartje said.

"It's not that simple," Etienne said.

"You don't have to be concerned, I have this under control," she said, calming her father somewhat.

Maartje stopped taking the drug. She found that she didn't need it as her tremors did not return. Unfortunately, her skating times began to diminish. Etienne began to wonder if the drug was really helping her skate faster.

"Maartje, we need to put you back on meldonium to see if your times improve," he said to her daughter.

"But Dad, that's cheating. If I am not good enough to win without it, then so be it," she said.

"But this is our dream. You've worked so hard for this." her father said. "I, ah, I mean, we have to have this."

"Dad, is there something you're not telling me?" Maartje

asked.

"We need the money from endorsements that you will get if you become a gold medal winner. I've gotten into some trouble. I owe a lot money to a bookie. I've been gambling. If I don't pay them, they said they are going to hurt me."

"Dad, how could you get involved with something like this?" Maartje asked.

"I have been depressed ever since your mother died last year. I kept this from you because I didn't want this to affect your training. I just got involved with the wrong crowd. But I don't bet on the horses anymore. I just need to pay this back."

"Oh Dad, how could you? What are we going to do?"

Etienne contacted Calvin at Test Me, LLC and had a conversation with the CEO. "Meldonium is now on WADA's banned substances list. My daughter was using your product very successfully. Now that the Winter Olympics is upon us in a few months, is there something else you can recommend that is not on the list?"

"I have just the thing," Calvin said.

When Etienne was told what it was, he agreed to give it a try. *This is so obvious that I should have thought of this myself,* Etienne thought. When the delivery came, he convinced Maartje that it was safe and that they should try it. When she was told what it was, she agreed. The drug came as a crystalline powder. The insert says, "Take one quarter teaspoon per day." It didn't take long for Etienne to know that this was working. Within a few weeks, Maartje's race times were as good as ever. They were convinced that she would be able to compete against the world's best, especially the Dutch women. Etienne's former opponent was now the women's national team coach.

*

I got a call from Dr. Larry Bowerman, a toxicology colleague of mine for many years. "I have a urine sample that I need for you to test," he asked me.

"Wait a minute, YOU are the head of the U.S. Anti-Doping Agency drug testing lab. You run one of the most sophisticated drug testing laboratories in the world. What do you need me for?"

"We have an athlete's urine who is abusing something that is not on our list. I needed for you to confirm the levels because we're not sure if it is real or an artifact. There are some other substances that appear to co-elute with the compound of interest." By co-elute, he meant that another drug present could have interfered with their test result.

"What is the drug?" I asked.

"I prefer not to say at this time," Larry said. "But don't worry, I know you test for it regularly."

We tested the material on the day it arrived. Based on our result, we were able to confirm Dr. Bowerman's suspicion. "Larry, what are you going to do with this information?" I asked.

"I need to consult with the Olympic Training Center's sports medicine docs on what recommendations they should make to the athlete before it is too late. What she is taking is not illegal but at these doses, it is particularly dangerous.

*

Three weeks before the US Olympic Trials, Etienne doubled up her dose. It seemed to energize her even more. A few days before the Olympic trials, she was ready to take on the world.

104

Before her preliminary heats, she was told to donate a urine sample while another woman watched her urinate. This was standard procedure, she had done this many times before, and therefore she was not embarrassed. Her father also told her that she had nothing to worry about. They would be clean. Later that afternoon, she went out for some practice runs. Her first race was in two days. After a few trial runs, she was back in the locker room where she became dizzy, had a headache and a fever. Later that night, alone in the hotel room, Maartje's heart started to beat uncontrollably fast. Then she had a seizure. Within a few minutes, she was unconscious. Her father entered her room and was not able to arouse her. When she arrived at the hospital she was already dead. Her body was sent to a coroner. Following an autopsy and toxicology tests, the cause was listed as an acute overdose of caffeine.

*

The World Anti-Doping Agency began testing for meldonium in September 2015, and added it to the list of banned substances effective January 1, 2016. Tennis star Maria Sharapova, formerly the world's number one female tennis player, failed a drug test for meldonium on January 26, 2016. She stated that she had been taking the drug under a doctor's supervision for the past 10 years because of irregular electrocardiograms, a deficiency in magnesium, and because of a family history of diabetes. She claimed that she was unaware of the ban until she received a letter from the International Tennis Federation during the 2016 Australian Open that her urine was positive for the drug. Sharapova lost to Serena Williams in the quarterfinals of that tournament. Her victories and the nearly $300,000 of winnings were forfeited. Given that she was once the wealthiest female athlete in the world, her disqualification will not dent her net worth. In June 2016, the ITF announced that Sharapova would be suspended from professional competition for two years. The ITF had considered a four-year ban but reduced it to two because of their belief that her use of the drug was not intended to improve her tennis performance. The five-time Grand Slam tennis winner stated that she would appeal the judgement. Given that 29-year old tennis star had suffered from a series of injuries causing her to miss several tournaments, her ability to regain the world's top tennis ranking is in jeopardy.

There have been several other elite athletes from Eastern European countries who have tested positive for meldonium and are facing a variety of sanctions. The list includes Ekaterina Bobrova, a Russian ice dancer in figure skating. She and her partner Dmitri Soloviev won the European Ice Dancing competition in 2013. Other athletes included those who participated in boxing, judo, mixed martial arts, wrestling, weight lifting, short track speed skating, cycling, biathlon, rugby, swimming, water polo bobsleighing, skeleton (sledding), and volleyball.

Meldonium is produced by Grindeks, a pharmaceutical company headquartered in Latvia and who have offices in 13 Eastern European countries. Is their main product, with sales in 2013 of 65 million euros. Meldonium is not approved by the FDA and is not available in the U.S. There are no scientific studies that have demonstrated that meldonium improves athletic performance. WADA's decision to include it on the list of banned substances was based on physiologic studies.

The Fountain of Youth

Nicole Jones came from a broken family. Her mother, Juliette, was a starlet in Hollywood who had an affair with a studio producer. When young, Juliette was blonde, pretty, and she had a great figure. She came from a small town in Texas and moved to Southern California in hopes of making it big on the silver screen. Her family begged her not to leave. They told her she wasn't pretty enough. But her ambition was just too great and she left when she was just 16 years old. Unfortunately, her producer boyfriend was only interested in her for sex and not in promoting her career. Juliette was one of thousands of attractive girls who would never make it in Hollywood. Their affair ended shortly after she announced to him that she was pregnant. Nicole was born and it was just the two of them for the first few years. Juliette continued to have many affairs but no one took her seriously.

In her early thirties, Juliette started to put on weight and her looks began to fade. This ended all of her acting opportunities. In order to support her daughter, Juliette became a waitress at a truck stop diner. The cook, Reuter, started dating Juliette. When Nicole was 9, she and her mother moved in with him. Reuter was a fatherly figure to Nicole. He could see that Nicole would grow up to be a real beauty and he was not shy about telling her that. On his off day when Juliette was working, Reuter took Nicole to the zoo, amusement parks, and sporting events. Soon, Juliette became jealous that Reuter was paying more attention to Nicole than to her. She and Reuter had a big fight over it and after 3 years of living together, Juliette and Nicole moved out. Reuter continued to see Nicole without her mother's knowledge. Reuter made Nicole feel good and he told her that her looks were a gift in this town. He taught her how to use her looks as an advantage around men. Tragically, Reuter died in a traffic accident when Nicole was seventeen. Nicole was devastated over the loss of the only father figure she ever had. By then she had grown up to be a stunningly beautiful young woman. She had long blonde hair, a perfect complexion, long legs and large breasts. She hired an agent and got steady work as a model in glamour magazine advertisements for cosmetics, clothes, and hair styling products. A few years later, Juliette died of ovarian cancer, so now Nicole was all alone in the concrete jungle of Los Angeles.

*

Carlos Avaya was a self-made millionaire. He opened a factory making women's clothes in Mexico when he was in his thirties. He learned very early that the key to success was to find a celebrity who would wear, model, and promote his outfits. He was lucky to find a young budding actress who agreed to be his spokesperson. When she became a star, she continued to promote Carlo's clothing line and his business became a huge success. Carlos worked well into his late 70s. He loved to be around young women and remained very involved with selecting the models his company used. Carlos interviewed Nicole to be one of their models and he was instantly attracted to her. After she was hired, Carlos started to come to many of her photo shoots. Nicole could tell that he liked her but she secretly thought, *he's old enough to be my grandfather.* The age difference didn't bother Carlos. One day after a shoot, Nicole was given a note by an aide. Carlos invited her to his mansion for a late night dinner. His driver picked her up from the studio and soon she and Carlos were alone. Carlos gave her a stunning diamond bracelet. They hugged, drank wine, talked some more, then after a few hours, he suggested they adjourn to his bedroom. Nicole wasn't sure he could have sex but she was a little drunk and didn't care if he couldn't get it up. But that thought was quickly dispelled. He was a caring and tender lover. Her original motivation in dating Carlos was to profit from knowing someone who was rich. She also needed a father figure like Reuter was to her. But later, she actually fell in love with the old guy.

Within a few years, Carlos at the age of 82 divorced his third wife of 20 years to marry Nicole, who was 27. The news media naturally thought that Nicole was only interested in his inheritance once he passed. Their marriage was a happy one despite the age difference. Carlos's two sons appeared to be happy for their father. The clothing company had been turned over to them many years earlier. Through the help of pharmaceutics, Nicole had two children with Carlos.

After 7 years of marriage, Carlos died of a cerebral hemorrhage. A few days after the funeral, Carlos' lawyer contacted the family to meet and disclose the terms of his will. While Nicole received a comfortable stipend that would allow her and her children to live comfortably for the rest of their lives, the bulk of the estate went to his sons. Nicole was crushed upon hearing this news. She rushed out of the room without speaking to her step children. She hired a lawyer for the purpose of contesting the will.

"He told me he wanted me to have a third of his estate. Those sons of his talked him into changing the will at the last minute," she told her lawyer. Nicole asked that the timelines of the will be thoroughly examined. After a few weeks, the attorney returned with his findings.

"The will appears to be in order. There was never any mention of you receiving 33% of his worth in any of the previous versions of the will. Did you sign a pre-nup or do you have anything in writing?"

"No, but he promised that he would take care of us," Nicole said.

"Apparently what you received was his definition of care. I found no evidence of mental incompetence. The last version was signed well before his death. I don't think we can win this case. My best advice is to not to contest this and be satisfied with the award you have. Those boys have a lot of money and can drag this case out for years or until your money runs out."

Nicole was not happy with this outcome but felt she had no choice. She was now in her mid-thirties and like her mother, her looks were beginning to fade along with her acting opportunities. She left the lawyers office not sure of her next step. *How can I stay young? Maybe it is time for plastic surgery?*

*

The success of Test-Me Inc. was life changing for Calvin. In the ten years since he and Barney formed the company, it had grown to 60 employees with a gross income of over $10 million per year. Having so much newly acquired disposable income, Barney taught Calvin how to live the dream. Calvin started wearing fancy clothes, driving fast cars, and dating "trophy" girlfriends. This was a far cry from when he was a lab jockey testing urine samples for a living. Each night, he went to the best nightclubs to see and be seen. To his credit, he stayed away from abusing drugs. Based on his current and prior work, he knew that the aging process accelerates for people addicted to crack cocaine and crystal methamphetamine. Their teeth rot out and their face and body become covered with blisters.

Calvin had the opposite attitude. He wanted to look younger and stronger, not old before his time. With this in mind, Calvin joined a gym and worked out every evening with free weights. Part of his motivation for working out was the incident in high school when Jaco pushed him into a bathroom stall. *This will not happen to me again,* Calvin vowed. Shortly after joining the gym, Calvin made some new friends. These were weight lifters, body builders, and professional trainers. They taught Calvin how to eat healthier by reducing unwanted fats and calories from his diet. He started taking vitamins, amino acids and protein supplements. He cut out the sugar drinks and carbonated beverages and he even gave up alcohol. Within a few months, his body began to lose body fat, which was replaced by solid muscle. His arms and chest enlarged. His waist shrank. His stamina increased. His employees could not believe how his body was being transformed. His confidence also soared. Calvin's clothes no longer fit and he needed a new wardrobe.

Most of the members at the gym knew what Calvin did

for a living. They accepted him as one of the guys just trying to look bigger and better. It was through their friendship that he learned about the dark side of body building. Some of the bigger men were competitive body builders. They entered local and regional fitness and physique contests.

During a conversation with Max, one of his gym friends, Calvin commented, "Look at Johnny over there. I've seen his workout regimen. It is not any more intense than ours. We all have trainers but his muscles are much more defined than ours."

Max looked at Calvin with a sideways stare but said nothing.

"Hey, I am not a guy who just crawled out from behind a rock," Calvin continued. "Do you know what he is taking?"

"Most of the other guys say it is anabolic steroids. But I am pretty sure it is growth hormone for Johnny Boy," Max replied. "His grandfather J.J. was a body builder and it was said that he used the stuff. Back then it was really hard to get so he had a definite advantage. "

Calvin went home and was determined to read up on J.J. He won many regional titles, and was runner up to the Mr. America in the 1960s. Growth hormone is a 191 amino acid peptide hormone that is produced by the brain's pituitary gland. This peptide stimulates cell growth and cell reproduction. In the late 1950s, growth hormone was extracted from the brains of cadavers. The peptide was purified and used to treat hormone-deficient children. Regular injections of this extract were successful in increasing the height of these little people by a few inches. During early clinical use, the science did not exist to produce this hormone in the laboratory. Therefore there was a growth hormone supply shortage, as it required pooling the pituitary extracts from many donors to provide enough for one injection. Thus the majority of dwarfs did not have access to the hormone. There were reports that some of the growth hormone supplies were stolen from endocrine centers that specialized in treating these children. *Did J.J. have access to stolen growth hormone? Was that how he got an advantage?* Calvin thought to himself while reading these articles. The truth will never be known. J.J. died prematurely of prostate cancer at the age of 34 years.

Calvin read that excess growth hormone stimulates insulin-like growth factor, known to be associated with increased risk for prostate cancer in men and breast cancer in women. Tall women have a higher breast cancer risk than short women, presumably due to higher circulating growth hormone levels. Calvin's next thought was how is the grandson, Johnny getting his growth hormone supply? Genentech in 1985 received FDA clearance for making growth hormone using a recombinant gene technique. Cadavers were no longer needed to get a supply! But the price was still very high and growth hormone was available only through a doctor's prescription. Calvin knew that the company charged a lot for it because of the expense incurred for research and development, and the costs needed to conduct clinical trials for FDA clearance.

Calvin decided that he wanted to get into the growth hormone supply business. He learned that any protein can be mass produced using recombinant DNA techniques if the amino acid sequence is known. Calvin felt he could sell his product to body builders at a greatly reduced price if it was part of an herbal preparation, thereby bypassing the normal FDA regulatory

113

approval process for drugs.

Calvin flew to Hong Kong and met with a friend who was making herbal supplements. Calvin knew that natural products were considered to be like foods and do not require FDA approval as a drug. *Growth hormone is a natural product, he reasoned.* So Calvin and Barney made plans to produce and sell the supplement. Recombinant protein production was outside of Calvin's prior scientific expertise. By then, he was much more involved with the business side of his company.

Cao read in the scientific literature about the commercial availability of cell cultures from rats that were engineered to produce human growth hormone. The trick was to keep the cultures alive so that a perpetual supply of protein can be extracted from the supernatant. Within a few months, these cells were producing viable hormones. They first tested the hormones on some rats.

"Human growth hormone has significant sequence homology to rodents," Cao explained to Calvin. The boss knew that what Cao meant was that the amino acid sequence between these species is very similar. "Published reports have shown that injection of human GH increases the rate of growth when compared to other rats that were not given growth hormone injections." A study was performed in their lab demonstrating that their growth hormone product appeared to be functional. More importantly, none of the hormone-treated rats died. Satisfied that it was not toxic, preparations of growth hormone were spiked into an herbal concoction. They called it "Bulk."

*

Nicole's agent found out about growth hormone and

suggested that if she wanted to stay young, she should begin using GH regularly. "This is a natural hormone that promotes healthy growth. It appears to slow the aging process. I know an herbal formulation of GH that is completely natural and safe. Do you want to try it?"

Nicole was excited about a non-surgical approach towards youth. She felt that plastic surgery could be an option for her many years from now, but that a natural product would be much less invasive. "This is great. Let's get it."

The agent purchased Bulk from Calvin's website and Nicole injected herself on a regular basis for the next few years. At first, the hormone was revitalizing. Nicole felt stronger and her skin appeared to be brighter. She figured if one dose was good, a double dose would be better, and then she increased it again. Her quest to maintain her beauty began to become an obsession. Soon, she noticed significant changes to her body. It began with her hands. The white gloves she used to use when she modeled formal clothing were now too small. She blamed the cleaners for shrinking them. In reality, her hands had increased in size. Then she noticed that her head was larger than before. Hats now no longer fit her head. Her jaw began to enlarge. These effects changed her from a pretty middle-aged woman to someone with facial disfigurements. Her agent pleaded for her to stop the injections. He showed her pictures of examples of before and after growth hormone abuse that were posted on the internet. Nicole was horrified that he could be so mean. Finally, convinced that growth hormone was causing her harm, she stopped taking the supplement. But by then, it was too late. Nicole developed bone cancer. Within a few months of diagnosis, the cancer had spread to her liver. While her doctors could not confirm that her cancer was due to growth hormone abuse, it was highly suspected. Nicole died of cancer 2 years after her diagnosis. She wanted to be buried next to Carlos but her step children would not allow it.

*

Anna Nicole Smith was a Playboy model, actress, and television personality. When she was 26, she married oil tycoon J. Howard Marshall, who was 89 at the time. Marshall died 14 months after their brief marriage. Neither Smith nor Marshall's oldest son, J. Howard Marshall III was included in $1.6 billion will. There were a series of lawsuits filed which all failed to overturn the terms of the Marshall's will. Anna Nicole died in 2007 due to "combined drug intoxication." There were many medications found in her body at the time of her death including chloral hydrate, diphenhydramine, and various tranquilizers (benzodiazepines). Although not listed as a cause of death, Anna Nicole Smith was also a frequent user of human growth hormone. She was allegedly taking this hormone to lose weight and to counteract the effect of aging.

Growth hormone deficiency during youth is associated with dwarfism and short stature. Excess secretion from the pituitary is associated with gigantism and is caused by a tumor that autonomously produces excess growth hormone. Robert Wadlow was the tallest man in recorded history, standing 8 feet 11.1 inches. Currently, Soltan Kosen from Turkey is the tallest living man in the world at a mere 8 feet 3 inches. Each of these giants suffered from an untreated tumor. Gigantism is relatively rare today because the disorder can be recognized and treated very early in life with surgery if the tumor is well defined, or through medication or radiation if the tumor is not well defined. Only in rural areas might a person reach puberty before gigantism is recognized and treated. Beginning with the 2016-17 season, the NBA will conduct three random drug tests on their basketball players for the presence of human growth hormone abuse.

Increased growth hormone secretion beginning in adulthood is associated with acromegaly. These individuals do not grow tall because the growth plates in their long bones have fused. But acromegalic patients suffer from abnormal bone growth in other areas. In this story, Nicole demonstrated the typical effects of acromegaly. Typically growth hormone abuse is not associated with a high degree of mortality. However, overuse is associated with a higher incidence of cancer and shorter life span. Nevertheless, growth hormone usage is on a sharp increase, with an estimated global market of over $4 billion per year.

Nicole's agent filed a complaint against the makers of Bulk. An investigation was conducted by the FDA who verified that it contained human growth hormone and that it was not a product that was derived from natural sources. The absence of safety data and production procedures and controls that are under tight FDA oversight made this formulation illegal. However, Calvin anticipated that eventually his fraudulently-labeled product would be discovered. The address for his product in China was fictitious. But just to be on the safe side, Calvin changed the location of the manufacturing facility every six months so that they could stay in business.

The Dope

****

Dr. Bert Goldman was the transfusion medicine director at my hospital when I began my training in laboratory medicine.

"What got you interested in blood banking when you were a pathology resident?" I asked him once when I was alone with him in his office.

"First of all, I am not a blood banker," he said rather emphatically. "While we do have a bank, I am director of Transfusion Services. We do much more than collect blood from donors. But the real answer is that blood is life. We have the power to restore life with a simple transfusion. But it can come at a price. Giving blood from someone else can be very dangerous."

Over the course of the next several months, I found out about the intricacies of the service and just how dangerous it is to get a unit. When someone donates a pint of blood, there is a lot of laboratory testing that goes on before that unit is ever given to anyone. Most people know about the importance of determining their blood type. The transfusion of an incompatible type can lead to a transfusion reaction that is very serious and potentially fatal. A unit of blood can also contain harmful viruses such as hepatitis or human immunodeficiency virus. Before certain laboratory tests were known, blood transfusions were a cause for the spread of hepatitis B, C and AIDS. Today, thanks to testing, the blood supply is much safer than it was a few decades ago, but the system is not 100% foolproof.

"This is why we are very cautious in releasing blood products to patients," Dr. Goldman told me. "The need to treat a bleeding or anemic patient must outweigh the risks for an infection." Today, transfusion-related acute lung injury or TRALI is a bigger issue than transmission of an infection. This occurs when blood from a donor causes an allergic reaction to the recipient resulting in lung injury. But this complication was unknown in the days of my fellowship training.

Dr. Bert Goldman had a son, Lenny, who was fascinated with transfusion medicine. As a child, he sometimes came into the lab to watch blood donations and to learn how testing was performed on collected units. He once accompanied his father when he performed a plasma apheresis procedure on a patient. This is a treatment whereby a machine replaces the plasma of a patient that contains harmful antibodies with plasma from a healthy donor. Lenny was not afraid of needles or the sight of blood.

Lenny was small for his age and because he liked to spend time in his father's hospital starting at 10 years of age, he was labeled as nerd. The neighborhood kids would tease him and sometimes steal his lunch money. Lenny learned to escape these hoodlums by jumping on his bike whenever he saw any one of the bullies coming. His love of the bicycle got him involved with local bicycle events. He often joined older riders in charity bike tours. They were 50 and 100 mile rides through the countryside.

The roads were roped off and there were regular rest stops with water and nutritional snacks. Lenny learned how to draft a group of fellow riders in order to conserve energy. He would lag behind a group of cyclists thereby reducing his wind resistance, enabling him to "coast" through at times without actively pedaling. Over the next few years, Lenny developed powerful thighs while maintaining a very slim figure and strong cardio vasculature. He started entering junior endurance races and began winning races even in the older age groups.

Upon graduation from high school, Lenny announced to his father that he was not going to college but was going to train full time with the junior national cycling team. Dr. Goldman was greatly disappointed with his son for not getting more education. But Lenny told his dad that he would enter college if his cycling career was a bust. So he left home and moved to the national cycling training center in Colorado Springs. While there, Lenny was exposed to the latest in equipment, training methods, nutrition, and even apparel and helmets. Lenny gradually moved up the ladder ahead of the other trainees but he was never the best. There were a few riders who were consistently better than him. He felt he needed an edge but he couldn't figure how to get it.

Then one day, it came to him. Through his father's work, he knew that blood transfusions were essential in treating anemic patients so that they could get the oxygen needed to meet their metabolic demands. What if he could increase his red cell mass by collecting and storing his own blood and then transfusing it just before a race? He went home and asked his father if he could participate in an auto-donation.

"What do you want your blood for?" Dr. Goldman asked. The doctor was not aware of any suspicious motive from his own son. Blood doping was not known in the profession then.

"Occupational hazard," he told his old man. "If I get into a bike crash and need emergency surgery, wouldn't it be better if I was transfused with a unit of my own blood? There will not be any incompatibility or infectious disease issues."

"That's very smart, son" Dr. Goldman told him. "But you will have to be extremely careful as to how it is labeled and stored. I will contact the blood bank in your city to ensure that the blood is labeled and stored correctly.

The transfusion was completed and the unit was labeled according to the current standards of the American Association for Blood Banks. The unit was placed into a special box, addressed to the blood bank in Colorado Springs and put into the overnight send-out area of the lab. Dr. Goldman said his goodbyes to his son and Lenny left the lab. But Lenny secretly came back to retrieve the blood bank package from the send-out area and he took it with him. Since the techs knew Lenny and had seen him over the years, nobody noticed or questioned what he was doing.

Lenny knew that this unit of blood was stable at refrigerated temperatures for up to 42 days, so he kept the blood in the back of his refrigerator. Lenny had planned this donation to coincide with a race that was scheduled in 2 weeks' time. A few days before the race, Lenny retrieved the unit, brought it to room temperature and proceeded to transfuse his own previously collected blood into himself in the privacy of his room. He had witnessed the procedure a few dozen times as a kid so he knew what he was doing. He had taken sterile tubing and needles from his father's lab before he left. The procedure took several hours and he did not transfuse the entire unit. When completed, he carefully discarded the empty bag and the associated tubing so that no one would know what he had done.

The race took place the next day. It was a 50-mile sprint. He lined up with the other racers and was ready to go. His split times for the first half of the race were similar to his other times. He thought to himself, *I see no benefit. This is not working.* But when he got to the final part of the race, where he would normally falter, he felt as strong as when he'd started. To the surprise of his teammates and the other racers, he sprinted the last 5 miles passing many of the other more seasoned riders. Lenny improved on his best time by over 4 minutes, a dramatic improvement in cycling. Over the ensuing months, Lenny continued to improve his performance to the point that he was now one of the top riders in the country. He regularly went back to his father to get blood transfusions stating each time that the previous unit had expired.

*

The success of Calvin's recombinant growth hormone business led him to ponder his next project for Cao and his staff.

"Erythropoietin is a naturally occurring hormone produced in the kidneys and it is used to treat patients with chronic kidney disease," he told Cao.

"It is also used to treat patients with anemia," Cao stated which took Calvin somewhat by surprise.

"So you have been reading up on this too?" the boss said

to the scientist.

"Sure have, boss-man. We can sell this stuff to endurance athletes. Marathon runners, long distance swimmers, cross country skiers, speed skaters, cyclists, weight lifters, mountain climbers...."

"Yeah, ok, I get it" Calvin said as he was getting up to leave.

But Cao continued. "Deep sea fisherman, astronauts, ballet dancers, rock musicians, transplant surgeons, ..."

"Wait, transplant surgeons?" Calvin asked

"Sure. Some of the procedures take 12-14 hours. You don't them want them to pass out?"

"I don't think so. Lets get to work." Calvin was thinking. *Well now, maybe it will help my golf game...*

Cao read the literature and found a procedure to produce EPO using a cell line from the ovary of a Chinese Hamster. Using the route that their company used for successfully producing and distributing growth hormone, Calvin and his company was soon selling recombinant EPO on the black market loosely disguised as an herbal supplement. They called it "Endurance."

*

Lenny's success led him to erythropoietin. By then, his teammates knew he was doping because he told them that the only way to win was to get a competitive advantage. But Lenny was not able to arrange for autologous blood bank donations by his teammates as he had done for himself.

"Why can't we use blood from an anonymous donor?" one of them asked.

"The lab can detect allogeneic cells by flow procedures" Lenny said. He then realized he was speaking in lab medicine jargon.

"And that means what?" another cyclist asked.

"Our red cells have a characteristic fingerprint. If we get transfused blood from someone else, these calls can be identified as being foreign by the clinical lab using a special instrument called a flow cytometer. Remember, I told you guys that these red cells circulate in our blood for 120 days. They are testing for this now so we would get caught."

The availability of Endurance facilitated widespread doping practices among his team, and a conspiracy in keeping their practices hidden. Soon, they were winning most of the national championships and many of the international events.

Under growing concern for doping, the International Cycle Association, the governing body for the sport, implemented random blood testing for hematocrit values. Being the son of a pathologist, Lenny knew all about the hematocrit.

"It is the volume percent of red cells in blood," he told his teammates when they learned about the new testing policy. "The normal hematocrit is about 45% for men." During Lenny's doping practices, his hematocrit exceeded 50%, which enable him to gain a competitive advantage. He now needed to carefully control his doping procedures.

The cutoff hematocrit limit was set at 50%. The athletes were regularly tested on a random basis. Testing for hematocrit discrepancies is a simple procedure that involves centrifugation of a blood sample. Lenny bought a used centrifuge from a laboratory warehouse and installed it in his apartment. Soon, he was regularly testing himself and all of his teammates. They all knew what their hematocrit was at any given moment. The group also learned the pattern and procedure for these random inspections. It was easy to spot the blood collectors when they arrived at the training center. They drove clearly marked cars identifying themselves. So there were always a few minutes of forewarning to the dopers before the inspectors appeared at the center. The doping cyclists planned that there would always be at least one person who was below the hematocrit cutoff. He would always be first to have his blood collected. In the meantime, the others were in the back room giving themselves injections of sterile saline, diluting the hematocrit to below the 50% limits and enabling them to pass. This scam worked for several years. They were never caught. Lenny, as the leader of the team, won numerous international cycling championships including the prestigious Tour of Rome.

Then in 2001, the ICA instituted blood and urine erythropoietin testing. But as ever the scientist, Lenny was not concerned.

"EPO is only present in our blood and urine for a few days, but the effects last for months." So unless blood collectors happen to catch us just after an injection, we will be safe from detection." Lenny also knew that humans naturally produced erythropoietin and the synthetic form produced by Calvin's lab was identical. He didn't know at the time that new lab procedures were being developed that would soon make this statement false. Lenny and his team continued to win international races for the next five years.

Lenny retired from active racing after his sixth

consecutive Tour of Rome Championship. He was an internationally known athlete who was constantly in the news. He began dating a former Olympic downhill skier that furthered his notoriety. Over the years, the International Cycle Association believed that Lenny and his team were doping but could not prove it. They had all of the blood and urine samples from Lenny's team frozen, waiting for sports medical science to catch up with the dopers. The ICA sponsored research grants in hopes of finding a laboratory test. Dr. Hans Schmidt of the Max Planck Institute was awarded one of the grants. Within a few years after Lenny's last championship, he discovered a means to differentiate between natural EPO and the one produced by artificial means. Using a technique known as isoelectric focusing, he found that the synthetic EPO was modified to contain carbohydrates that attached to the protein. These are not found in the native protein. Using this technique, Dr. Schmidt was able to differentiate the foreign EPO from the one our bodies produce naturally

Without permission from athletes, the ICA commissioned testing of all of the samples collected on Lenny and his team mates during their Tour of Rome competitions. They were hopeful of finally finding the evidence they needed to prove that they cheated during these races. Unfortunately, recombinant EPO is only remains for a maximum of a week so none of these samples were positive. Just to be absolutely sure, some of the data were sent to independent scientists who were knowledgeable about sports doping procedures, including myself. The data was de-identified by the ICA. I didn't know that it included the son of my former colleague. I received a set of computer printouts and data to see if the German scientists might have missed something. Unfortunately for the ICA, my review concurred with those of Dr. Schmidt. It looked like Lenny and his team would escape detection once again.

The ICA, however, was committed to convict Lenny. They contacted several of his former team mates and presented them with the data. Knowing that they would not be able to interpret the results, some of the attorneys told them that this data was absolute proof. But the ICA wanted all of the details of how the team deceived the testers for future use, so they offered amnesty to each of the team members who were willing to come clean. They also threatened to expose them to their sponsors which could have resulted in convictions for practices intended to fraudulently obtain their financial support. Armed with these threats, most of Lenny's team confessed that they along with their leader were doping.

Lenny continued to deny any involvement with doping, calling his former teammates liars. He was intent on keeping his Tour of Rome titles. He didn't believe the Union had direct evidence of doping and it was his word against the others. He went on the national and international media denying the allegations and attacked the Union. It looked like it would be an ugly drawn out affair costing millions of dollars for all concerned. But at the last minute, Lenny called Barbara Williams, a well-known television interviewer of celebrities. The interview was scheduled for live TV. Having Sarah, his beautiful and athletic skier girlfriend standing next to him during the interview simply added to the spectacle:

"Barbara: Lenny, the world wants to know. Are you guilty of doping?

Lenny: "Yes. I am tired of fighting these charges. I admit to lying to the investigators. I admit to using performance enhancements. I want to move on from here."

Barbara: "Why are you coming forward today?"

Lenny: "This has been a witch hunt from the very beginning. I am being singled out only because I won. But almost everyone else in the sport was doping also. So the playing field was level, as far as I could tell."

Barbara: "Do you have any proof of this allegation?"

Lenny: "No, but it is common knowledge among the athletes. I don't have any more proof than what the ICA has on me."

Barbara: "Aren't you setting a bad example for the youth of this world?"

Lenny: "There is something wrong if I am the role model for your children. Their parents should be their role models. I cannot be held responsible for what your child will do. I say to them now, don't follow my actions. Create your own path. I did what I felt I had to do to succeed."

Barbara: "If you could go back, would you do it the same way again?"

Lenny: "Without hesitation. I was nothing before I won these events. I was just a kid who was picked on. Now you can put my name with the very best in sports. Basketball, Michael Jordan. Golf, Tiger Woods. Hockey, Wayne Gretzky.
Barbara: But none of them cheated."
Lenny: "That we know of."

Barbara: "You're not accusing them of cheating are you?"

Lenny: "No, I have no knowledge one way or the other."

Barbara: "Haven't you lost all of your endorsements?"

Lenny: "My net worth is in the millions. Yes, I traded my soul to the devil. But there are hundreds of others who would do the same. Many are doing it right now. We just don't know about them."

Barbara: "What about your relationship with Sarah? How will this be affected?"

Lenny: "I have discussed this with her already and she is behind me 100%. She knows it was a means to an end."

The interview ended a few minutes later and Barbara thanked her guest. After he left the room, she said to her producer, "Boy what an asshole."

The producer said, "Yea, nobody feels sorry for what happened to him."

*

Calvin was watching the interview on television at his home knowing full well that it was his product that Lenny and the others had used. A decade ago, he was intent on catching cheaters. Today, he is the facilitator of such actions.

I was watching the interview from home. I remembered Lenny as a kid who visited the clinical lab frequently. Dr. Goldman died a few years before Lenny's national prominence and was spared the family's humiliation. But it was clear that Lenny was not remorseful in any way for his actions.

*

This story is a fictitious departure from the events of Lance Armstrong, who was investigated by the U.S. Department of Justice and the U.S. Anti-Doping Agency. These investigations ended with his disclosure of guilt on the Oprah Winfrey show in January, 2013. Part of his motivation for telling the truth was to allow his charitable foundation to survive the storm. Armstrong was a survivor of testicular cancer prior to his victories in the Tour de France. The objective of the Lance Armstrong Foundation that was formed in 1997, was to inspire and empower cancer survivors, just as he had done. The Foundation changed its name to Livestrong in hopes of continuing their mission despite Armstrong's doping disclosure. Livestrong continues to make significant contributions to cancer research despite Armstrong's downfall.

Armstrong was a role model to any child who a rode bicycle. But it was Charles Barkley in a Nike commercial who stated that he was not a role model for children, encouraging parents and teachers to step up.

Exogenous EPO administration can be detected by our modern laboratory procedures, but because the hormone has a short half-life, there is a very narrow window by which blood and urine must be collected. Moreover, there are other chemicals and drugs that activate the erythropoietin gene in producing more red cells. Therefore, the focus for doping practices among athletes remains on measuring the outcome of red cell production by the bone marrow, and not of the stimulants themselves. Some scientists have developed algorithms that combine red cell parameters with other markers. The reticulocyte count is a measure of immature red cells that have higher oxygen carrying capacity. The soluble transferrin receptor participates in iron metabolism. Both are increased with regular EPO use. Unfortunately, none of these measurements are 100% conclusive. This is because humans have significant biological variation between us, meaning that some "outlier" individual may naturally have abnormal levels. Therefore doping practices continue in various competitive sports.

There are significant medical dangers for overuse of erythropoietin. Increasing the hematocrit thickens the blood, retarding its normal flow, especially at night when the heart rate is reduced. Thick blood has a higher tendency to form clots. When these form in the heart or brain, the end result is a heart attack or stroke. Between the years of 2003 and 2004, seven elite European cyclists, ranging from 16 to 35 years died mysteriously. Two of them died in their sleep, while another had just left the dentist's office. Some individuals in the racing community have wondered if EPO abuse was responsible for their deaths. Marco Pantani of Italy, who won the 1998 Tour de France and was alleged to be on EPO, also died during this time. But cocaine was found on post mortem analysis and this and not EPO was listed as the cause of his death.

Footlights

On that night, DeJon worked the third shift at the livery. His last pickup at the airport was for Mrs. Harry Selig, who was flying alone from New York to San Francisco. It was rainy and cold and the flight was delayed 2 hours. Everyone is inconvenienced when planes come in late. Cab drivers can just go home; someone else can pick up the fares. But nobody thinks about the limousine drivers. They just sit in their cars listening to their radios. Passengers embarking from late flights are always grumpy. This is especially true of the business executives who take limo drivers for granted. Their rides are prepaid by their company. So they usually don't tip drivers, even if the drivers get stuck waiting hours for their plane to arrive.

Brianna was coming home after spending yet another unhappy weekend with her husband in the Big Apple. As the chief engineer for his company, he was there on an important construction job supervising the installation of the building elevators. She was tired of these cross-country flights. Just before she left, she had a big fight with him.

"I told you that you shouldn't have taken this job," she told him. "Why do I have to be the one to sacrifice for this marriage all the time? You are never home, and I am getting tired of these long trips. God knows what you do when I am away."

"Just a few more months now, honey, and my part of the job will be all over," her husband Harry replied in an attempt to console her.

"Then you will be off to another part of the country and onto the next job. Something has got to change!"

She boarded the plane and didn't look back. When she was out of sight, Harry got into a cab and pulled his cell phone out of his pocket. He punched the number 2 on the speed dial list. At least Brianna's phone number was speed dial number 1. The person at the other end answered immediately. He then said to her, "She's gone. You can come over now."

When Brianna arrived at SFO, she dragged her carry-on luggage downstairs to the baggage claim area. She was still wearing a light blue gown from the dinner she and Harry had earlier that night. DeJon was wearing his chauffeur's outfit and had a sign with her name on it. Brianna saw the sign and went over to the driver.

"I'm Mrs. Selig," she said without making eye contact with the driver. "No checked bags. Let's go." She gave him the handle of her wheeled luggage and they proceeded out the door. She had been through this drill before and knew where the limos were parked and walked ahead of the driver. He pulled out his paperwork to remind him of their destination. It was in the city of Atherton, a high-end suburb of San Francisco, on the peninsula between SF and San Jose.

As she walked, there was something about her that was familiar to DeJon. *I know I've seen that face before.* It took him a few minutes, but when she got into the back of the limo, he said something. "Don't we know each other?" he asked her.

For the first time, Brianna looked at the driver. He had a beard, mustache and his hair was unkept. "I am sure you are mistaken," she said. There was no way she would every go out with a man like that.

DeJon drove in silence down route 280 toward their destination and they didn't say anything more for the first half of the trip. But as she sat there, she finally remembered. It all came back in a rush. She leaned forward and tapped the driver on the right shoulder. "You're DeJon, aren't you?" she said.

"How are you Brianna?" It had been 25 years since they parted. She was going to be a singer. He was the high school's basketball team star. Her goal was Hollywood. He was being recruited to play basketball at Duke University.

*

Brianna and DeJon were from the opposite sides of the track. Brianna's father owned a real estate company. They was one of the first African American families to live in Atherton, a wealthy suburb near Stanford University. DeJon was from the low rent district of East Palo Alto. They met at a party in high school. They were together as a couple for a brief period of time in their senior year of high school. It was Brianna that introduced DeJon to the Chinese herb called "ma huang." She was taking it as an aid to lose weight. But she heard from friends that the herbal was also useful to enhance athletic performance.

"Duke Basketball is a religion in North Carolina," Brianna said. "If you get in, you will be revered as a god. It might not be a bad idea to get an edge wherever you can find one."

"But is it safe?" he asked her.

"I've been taking it for years and it hasn't affected me. Don't I look gooood?" Brianna said, taking off her sweater and then striking a pose for DeJon to see.

DeJon's eyes lit up. He scanned her figure from head to toe. Brianna could see that he liked her. They kissed and soon they were in bed together for the first and only time. Thereafter, DeJon began taking ma huang during the basketball season. He noticed that his body temperature appeared to increase soon after taking this herb. But he wasn't concerned. It seemed to make his breathing easier and improved his endurance during basketball drills.

*

I came to the General just shortly after some of my new colleagues in lab medicine and pharmacology completed a study on ephedra. I learned that toxicology studies are case-based, because it is unethical to conduct a randomized trial on a potential intoxicant. Dr. Christine Haller was the lead scientist in this study on ephedra alkaloids.

"How can you demonstrate causation from case reports, however detailed they are?" I asked her. "Drug levels in blood are usually not available."

"Since we can't give a drug that we think might be toxic and collect blood, the next best thing we can do is to see in these reports, if symptoms subside when the subject stops taking the drug and if they recur when they are reintroduction to it. "If symptoms do recur, it should be within a timeframe that is consistent with the drug's pharmacology." I knew that pharmacokinetic data include how long drugs last in the body. Such data were conducted on human volunteers and published prior to their release into clinical usage. While there was no data for the herbal ephedra, the active ingredient was ephedrine and pseudoephedrine, which are present in over-the-counter cold medications.

In Dr. Haller's analysis of subjects who reported toxicities to the FDA while on these supplements, she concluded that half were either definitely or probably related to consuming supplements containing ephedra, while the other cases were indeterminant. Death, stroke and other permanent medical disability occurred in many of these subjects, even in the absence of any preexisting conditions or concurrent risks. In some cases, the dose used by these individuals was less than the amount typically used for pseudoephedrine to treat asthma. But ma huang and other products contained several amines that may have a collective effect. Dr. Haller's work was published in the *New England Journal of Medicine.* I make it required reading for all of my toxicology students today.

*

DeJon had his best season as a senior. He played the power forward position and averaged 17 points and 10 rebounds per game. He was listed on Parade Magazine's All American High School Basketball Team. DeJon was awarded scholarships from many colleges including Duke. It helped that DeJon was an above average student and smarter than most of the jocks attending his high school. He signed a letter of intent to play for the Duke Blue Devils in Durham, North Carolina. He was excited to leave his home. He had never been outside the State of

California, let alone seen the Atlantic Coast.

"You are going to have to get into better shape to play for Duke," DeJon's coach told him. He was very proud of the boy's achievement. The coach asked the school's trainer to work with DeJon over the summer. Together, they put together a rigorous schedule of calisthenics, aerobic exercise, and weight training. His diet was also improved to optimize physical performance. Toward the end of the summer, he converted 10 pounds of fat to pure muscle. He was ready for the start of school, but he wanted one more rigorous session with the trainer. It was outdoors and very warm in Northern California that day....

*

Brianna first began singing in her church choir. During her senior year in high school, she got the lead role of Ester Hoffman in the musical, *A Star is Born*. But it was not a harbinger of good things to come for Brianna. With the help of her family, Brianna went to Hollywood and hired an agent hoping to get roles on stage, film, or television. African Americans were beginning to get prominent parts when she arrived to Tinsel Town. But it was not to be for her. She was propositioned by producers many times in exchange for small roles, but she refused all advances. After 5 unsuccessful years, she left the profession and returned to Northern California. She appeared in a handful of commercials and as a backup singer but otherwise she went unrecognized. Back home, she met Harry Selig, a construction company engineer. They married and moved to a big house in the Pacific Heights region of San Francisco. The first few years of the marriage were happy ones for Brianna. They tried to have children but were unsuccessful. It wasn't clear if there were problems with Brianna or her husband. Their marriage suffered as a consequence. Selig began secretly seeing other women and cheating on his wife. Brianna saw that Selig was losing interest in her and he had his eye on younger women.

On the practice field, DeJon was doing a series of wind sprints. The trainer had a stopwatch in his hand and was pushing DeJon to run faster.

"The college game is much faster than in high school. You will be running up and down the court. Don't let Coach K see you out of shape or you won't get playing minutes."

DeJon was hot and exhausted. He drank water in between the sprints but it was apparently not enough. At the end of the series, be bent over with his hands on his knees. He was sweating profusely and breathing hard. Then he keeled over lying face up on the ground and began seizing. The trainer rushed over to him. DeJon was suffering from heat stroke. The boy was rushed to the hospital. He never told the trainer that he was regularly taking ephedra. His temperature in the emergency department was 105°F. The ER staff removed his clothes and he was put into an ice bath to reduce his core temperature.

DeJon suffered a cardiac arrest and was transferred to the intensive care unit where he remained for the next several weeks. Urine was collected, and sent to my laboratory for a drug screens. The positive screen prompted confirmatory analysis using mass spectrometry. The next day, we reported to the doctors the presence of ephedrine in his urine sample.

DeJon's cardiac arrest caused serious damage to his heart. His troponin was markedly increased. We also noted that the enzyme creatine kinase was one thousand times higher in his blood than normal. It was so high that the techs had to do multiple dilutions to keep the result on scale. DeJon suffered from a condition known as "rhabdomyolysis." With his fever and high blood pressure, his muscles began breaking down. A big man to begin with, the destruction of his muscles led to an acute failure of his renal function. He was treated with dialysis which removed the toxins and enabled his kidneys to recover.

His doctors told him that he would likely not be able to play college basketball. The athletic department at Duke University was informed. They kept his scholarship by red-shirting him during his freshmen year in hopes that he could play the following year. After a few months, DeJon got back onto the basketball court trying to muster a comeback. But after even a light workout under the watch of an assistant coach, he developed chest pain and had to stop. A few months later, he announced to his family and friends that he was giving up on his basketball career. His scholarship was not renewed and DeJon was forced to drop out of school after the first year.

Back home, DeJon was in a depression for many years thereafter. He had difficulty focusing or maintaining a job. Dejon also went through periods of homelessness and drug abuse. He never married. Then while he was in his late thirties, he walked into a cab company looking for work. The interviewer attended the same high school as DeJon.

"Weren't you DeJon, the star of our basketball team?" he asked.

"I'm still Dejon, but I am out of roundball now. I got hurt and had to quit."

"We'd love for you to work for us." DeJon abstained

from drugs for the next week in order to pass his drug test. He was offered a job as a driver. The former basketball star was appreciative of the job offer, cleaned up his act, and was an exemplary driver for many years.

*

It was sad for DeJon to see Brianna in his taxi on that cold and rainy night. Neither of them achieved the goals they set out to achieve so many years ago. Brianna said that they must get together but DeJon knew it would never be arranged. Brianna gave him a $100 dollar bill for a $25 dollar fare. Another man might have been insulted. Another man might not have let her go in the first place. But he was resigned to his circumstance and simply put the bill into his pocket. Brianna walked out of the cab with her head down. She walked slowly to her house and didn't look back. DeJon waited a minute and then drove off.

*

The active ingredients of ephedra are ephedrine and pseudoephedrine. These compounds are termed "sympathomimetic amines." They act on the body to raise blood pressure and expand the lungs to make breathing easier. The effect of ephedra on athletic performance is unproven. Ephedrine has a similar structure to methamphetamine and is used as an important starting material in illegally producing this drug for street use.

The work of Haller and Benowitz was instrumental in convincing the FDA to ban the sale of ephedra-containing supplements in 2004. But this was too late for several noteworthy professional athletes. Both Kory Stringer, an offensive lineman for the Minnesota Vikings and Steve Bechler, a pitcher for the Baltimore Orioles died of complications from heatstroke during workouts in 2003. Both professional athletes were taking ephedra at or near the time of their deaths, although postmortem toxicology results on Stringer were negative for the presence of any supplements. During hearings from the Department of Justice, one of the companies making ephedra was ordered to disclose their reports of over 15,000 ephedra-related adverse events, including many deaths. The co-founder and the owner of Metabolife were both convicted in a federal court for failing to report these deaths to the FDA and for income tax evasion.

Today ephedrine and pseudoephedrine are still available without prescription. However, the U.S. Drug Enforcement Administration has required drug stores to keep the product behind the counter. The amount that can be sold is limited each month. Buyers must present photo identification to purchase products containing pseudoephedrine and records of purchases are maintained by the pharmacy for at least two years.

DeJon was not the only high level basketball player to play with kidney failure. Sean Elliott of the San Antonio Spurs played one full season following a kidney transplant from an organ he received from his brother. Elliott retired in 2001 after 12 seasons in the National Basketball Association with a career scoring average of 14 points per game. Elliott's renal failure was not the result of taking herbal supplements. Today, the former small forward is a television analyst for professional and college basketball.

Many readers will recognize this story as being similar to Harry Chapin's song, Taxi, about Harry and Sue, who once dated and coincidently meet in Harry's cab many years later. Like Brianna and DeJon, neither of them had fulfilled their dreams. However, Chapin wrote and sang a more pleasant sequel to Taxi ten years later where the driver becomes a radio DJ and the girl leaves her husband and her unhappy former life. But he still doesn't get the girl and he ends the song with the line, "I guess only time will tell." This opened the door for a sequel to the sequel. But it didn't happen for Chapin. A year later, the singer/song writer died in a traffic accident.

.

Gonadal Blues

"This has to be a mistake in the labeling of the sample" when Millie, my lab tech was saying as she presented me with a request for hCG on a male patient." hCG is human choriogonadotropin and is produced by the placenta during pregnancy. When positive in blood or urine, it usually indicates pregnancy, however, persistently positive results in the absence of pregnancy can also be produced by gestational tumors. This is a serious condition with a significant mortality rate. Treatment requires surgery, chemotherapy, and/or radiation therapy.

"Yes, it is true that normally we test hCG only on women but there are some other explanations for why testing is conducted in men," I told Millie. "hCG is produced in a minority of men who have testicular cancer." As part of our quality assurance program for the clinical laboratory, it is within my purview to review cases such as these to determine if an error in labeling has occurred. It was also remotely possible that our patient is labeled as a male because this person is in the process of changing their gender and was born a female. Even in the absence of pregnancy, healthy women can have measurable hCG levels, especially those who are postmenopausal. But the age and sex were listed as an 18-year old male. We found a strongly positive result for hCG, well beyond the value we expected in a healthy female. I found out who the attending physician was from the order entry system and placed a call. The lifetime odds of getting testicular cancer are one in 270 men. The age range of between 20 and 34 years did fit the patient's demographic. But after talking to the doctor, this was not the reason for why he ordered the test.

*

Clay Duffel was pushed into baseball from an early age by his father. Horace Duffel was a promising minor league pitcher who blew out his elbow while pitching for the Cedar Rapids Kernels, minor league A team in Iowa. His pitching motion was such that he threw the ball while his elbow was above the shoulder. This led to regular arm and elbow problems. He eventually underwent Tommy John surgery on his pitching elbow to reconstruct his elbow. Tommy John was a pitcher for the Chicago White Sox and was the first professional baseball player to have this surgery performed. But Horace lost too much velocity on his fastball as a result of the surgery and he was out of baseball the following year. He devoted his time to the development of his only son, Clay. Horace's wife was also a good athlete having played college basketball. Both she and Horace were over six feet tall, so they naturally assumed that Clay would also be taller than average and potentially a gifted athlete. Horace hoped that Clay would become a professional ball player, but his Dad warned him very early in his development.

"I don't want you to become a pitcher like I was," he told Clay when the boy was playing in the Little League. "If you get any arm trouble, your career could be over before it really starts."

"Dad, what do you mean, career? I'm not going to be a baseball player, I just want to have fun with some of my friends," Clay said. Harold got the message. If he pushed his son too hard, it could backfire and he might hate the game. So while Harold attended every game, he didn't put any pressure on his son to succeed. *This will have to come from his own desire,* he reasoned. The plan worked. Clay did become interested in the game and worked hard at it. He was the starting left fielder for the high school team. They took second in the state championships during his senior year. Clay was tall at 6 foot 3 inches, but very thin, weighing only 180 pounds. His coaches tried to get him to bulk up through diet, but Clay had a fast metabolism and could not gain weight. He was drafted out of high school by the New York Mets organization but he turned down the offer electing to play college baseball. Clay had a distinguished college career, and was drafted again after his senior year, but this time to the Boston Red Sox. He joined Boston's Greenville Drive A minor league team shortly after graduating from college. His minor league coach also told Clay that he would be a better player if he were stronger and heavier. Clay wanted to be a major leaguer at some point. He did some reading and took matters into his own hands.

*

Calvin and his team of scientists observed that male athletes had begun using hCG. He did some investigations as to the physiologic effect that this female hormone had on athletic performance. Convinced that there was a market for this product, Calvin asked his production team if they could get into the hCG production business. But his growth hormone and erythropoietin demands had pushed their production capacity to the limit. Cao's time was consumed with meeting Barney's sales quota and it could not be diverted toward a new project. So, if Calvin wanted to offer hCG, he had to find another way to get a supply of the hormone that didn't require Cao's recombinant DNA expertise. It was Barney's pregnant girlfriend, Bonnie, who offered the solution.

"There is a ton of hCG that is excreted into the urine of pregnant women." Bonnie learned that from her obstetrician." Why don't you extract it from my urine and from the pregnant girls in the office?"

"Sometimes the most obvious solution is sticking out right in front of our noses," Calvin said to her as he was staring at Bonnie's inflated tummy. Calvin found an extraction procedure from the literature and hired a chemistry student from a local college to process urine obtained from these women. Within a few days, they had a supply of purified hCG. Once a supply was produced and sterilized, they needed a way to test its effectiveness.

"Determining the concentration of hCG in the preparation is easy," Calvin, the former clinical laboratory tech, said to his hCG group. "We can spike some of the preparation into a serum sample devoid of hCG and send it off to a clinical laboratory for testing." Calvin left instructions on how to prepare the sample and it was sent to a clinical laboratory. The result came out strongly positive for hCG. While this proved that the hormone was present, it doesn't prove that the hCG was biologically active in stimulating the ovaries.

"Maybe the extract deactivated the hormone even if it is detected by the laboratory test," Calvin told his group. "So we have to do the rabbit test."

"What does that mean?" one of his techs asked.

"Many years ago, pregnancy was determined by injecting the urine of a woman suspected of being pregnant into a female rabbit. If hCG was present in the urine sample, it would cause an enlargement of the ovaries."

"I've heard about this. If the rabbit dies, the woman is pregnant," the tech said.

"Not quite," Calvin explained. "In order to examine the ovaries, all of the rabbits had to be sacrificed to look for ovarian masses. Thanks to the hCG test, nobody does this anymore."

Calvin's lab had the certifications needed from the Animal Welfare Committee to obtain experimental rabbits. Calvin's hCG preparations were injected. Within a few days, each of the test animals exhibited the changes that were expected, relative to the animals whom were given unspiked urine alone. Satisfied that the hormone was functional, they followed the same herbal model of marketing their other products, claiming that their formulation was based on natural ingredients and was useful for improving fertility health. In a sense, their marketing was not wrong. These were naturally derived hormones that were not manufactured or concocted. They called their product "Life." But in reality, they were targeted towards the athletic performance enhancement market.

*

In order to increase his bulk for baseball, Clay purchasing testosterone supplements from his local drug store and didn't tell his parents about it. He was entering his senior year in high school. He read warning labels and internet articles and was concerned that long-term testosterone use would shrink his testicles and curb his libido. Testosterone, like many hormones in the body, operate on a feedback system. The injection of testosterone causes the brain to send signals to the testes to shut down the natural testosterone production. *Overtime, my balls will shrink!* Clay thought to himself. Not wanting that to happen, he read about how he could prevent it through the administration of human choriogonadotropin. This hormone stimulates the testes to produces testosterone, thereby preventing testicular atrophy. Through the black market, Clay purchased hCG from Calvin's lab.

In order to prepare himself for the spring baseball season, Clay started a rigorous weight training and exercise program in the fall semester. The testosterone enabled him to workout longer. After six months of regular testosterone and hCG use, Clay began to see significant differences in his body. He gained 30 pounds of muscle. He was no longer the skinny kid his friends and family knew. He also noticed that his baseball cap had to be expanded to fit his head, and he began to develop significant acne on his face and back. His mother helped him with the acne through the purchase of creams. His father noticed that his son was bigger but he just thought that it was the result of natural growth and maturity. Horace, after all, was bigger than the average man.

When Clay's last year of high school baseball season began, he was a different player. His arms were stronger, he ran faster, but most importantly, he could hit the ball with much more power than ever before. He dramatically increased the number of home runs and other extra base hits over last year's total. The coaches put him in the clean-up spot in the lineup, resulting in more RBI opportunities. Within a few games, it became evident that Clay was clearly the best hitter on the team and possibly in their entire league. Unlike many power hitters who have an upper cut swing which results in long and high fly balls, Clay's swing was a level plane. His batted balls would rocket off his aluminum bat as line drive missiles.

The team's third-base coach, Amid Johnson, especially took notice of the boy's power. Foul balls hit by him would whiz by the coach's head along the third baseline, forcing him to duck on a regular basis. It got to the point that Coach Johnson began to wear a batting helmet while standing in the coach's box. Some of the other coaches and fans began kidding him about this practice, since none of the other coaches wore helmets before. He responded to these hecklers by saying, "Hey, the fielders have gloves out there. And they are young and have fast reflexes. I'm just a sitting duck."

But Coach Johnson was wrong in thinking that the players were safe. During one game, Clay hit a ball directly back to the pitcher. Phil and Clay used to play sandlot baseball together as kids and they were now rivals on their high school team. But on this day, Phil was not able to put his glove up fast enough and Clay's batted ball struck Phil squarely on the forehead. Phil fell straight backwards and lay unconscious on the pitching mound. Both teams rushed out to the mound to help the fallen player. An ambulance was called and Phil was still out when he was taken to the local emergency department. The boy became conscious while in the hospital but was groggy for many hours. He suffered a serious concussion and was admitted to the pediatric intensive care unit. Clay visited his friend each day while he was in the hospital. Phil made a full recovery and was discharged after three days. But the event ended any hopes of Phil's continuing in baseball. He could never again face another hitter without the fear of getting hit again. He didn't blame Clay for what happened. They both knew it was all part of the risk of the game and they remained friends.

Horace had never seen a ball hit that hard before, even in the professional leagues and he confronted his son. "Are you using PEDs?" he demanded shortly after the last game. Clay knew that PEDs meant performance enhancing drugs.

"Absolutely not," he said, lying to his father. "You've always wanted me to play baseball, and now that I am good at it, you think I am not good enough. But I am. You'll see." Clay left the room without saying anything more.

Horace could not challenge his son any longer without the risk of alienating his young impressionable son further. He sought another means to find out. Horace knew that Clay was scheduled to see the family doctor regarding a physical exam he needed in case he went to college. Clay was hoping to get a tryout and a contract with a minor league team, but if that fell through, he would accept one of the many college scholarships he received that spring to play baseball. Horace called Dr. Chan's office and they met in the doctor's office a few days before Clay's scheduled physical.

"I think my son is enhancing his baseball skills by taking supplements. You will see when he visits that his body has changed dramatically since your last exam. Can we do some lab testing to verify this? I have confronted him but he has denied any involvement."

"Testing for supplements such as steroids requires a specialized lab, and I really cannot justify that without his permission," remarked Dr. Chan.

"But he is a minor, can't I request it?" Horace asked.

"It is really not ethical without his knowledge. Besides, we can't get insurance to pay for this test. But I could order a testosterone and hCG to see if they are normal" Dr. Chan said. "If he is taking testosterone, it might be abnormally high."

"I know what testosterone is but what is hCG?" Horace asked.

"This is a hormone that stimulates the ovaries and testes. Athletes who abuse anabolic steroids have reduced testosterone production. The use of hCG helps to restore some of their natural testosterone production. These tests are also used to check for the presence of testicular cancer. This could be part of the workup for this problem."

Dr. Chan ordered the tests and they were sent to my laboratory. Both the testosterone and hCG result were increased above the normal range. Dr. Chan called Horace to discuss the results.

"I think you were right. There is evidence that Clay is using performance enhancement drugs. If you want, I can discuss the medical dangers of this practice. He should stop immediately. What he is trying to accomplish is not worth risking his health."

"As a former professional athlete myself, I will speak to my son about this," Horace said. "I'll let you know if I need help." He thanked the doctor, hung up the phone, then called his wife and briefed her on his suspicions, and together they went into Clay's room.

When told of what his father had done, Clay was outraged. "You have no right to interfere. This is my body and my life. I don't care what the medical risks are. I know what I am doing. I won't give this up. It has made a difference. There will be pro scouts at my next game. Don't wreck this for me, Dad. I will never forgive you." With that, he demanded that his parents leave his room. Horace could see that there was nothing he could do to change the situation. Their son was going to be leaving soon and he wanted to have some relationship to build on. He secretly told his wife that he hoped Clay didn't get a minor league contract so he could lead a somewhat normal life as a college student athlete.

The next game, Clay got 2 hits after three at bats with a double, home run, one long fly out, and two intentional walks. The scouts were impressed with his power. The scout from the Baltimore Orioles told him that he would be high on their draft list. On draft day, Clay's name was announced during the second round. With the help of his father, Clay hired an agent and they met with the Orioles to sign a contract. He got a lucrative signing bonus and was assigned to the team's A farm team, the Dalmarva Shorebirds of Salisbury, Maryland. Clay sent out letters to the colleges rejecting their admission and scholarship offers and joined the minor league team shortly after high school graduation.

After signing the contract, and in order to pass the urine drug test, Clay stopped using testosterone and hCG. He knew he had to be more careful in using this supplement. He did not want to be suspended by the minor leagues before his season began in earnest. But after he passed his first drug test, Clay went back on the juice. This time, he supplemented the testosterone with epitestosterone, an inactive hormone that is co-produced with testosterone. Clay learned that the league measured the ratio of testosterone to epitestosterone. When this calculation was high, that is greater than 6 to 1, it indicated external testosterone supplementation. By taking epitestosterone, he was normalizing this ratio. Clay also restarted hCG, which further increased his natural testosterone and epitestosterone production, in an attempt to hide his abuse.

All went well for Clay during the first few months of the minor league season. He had little problem adjusting to the speed of the minor league game. Pitchers were a little faster and they were throwing sharper breaking balls but he was successful in hitting them and maintained a good average during the first few months of the season. Clay had to get used to wooden bats as the aluminum sticks were not allowed.

Most of the other players on Clay's team were older, married, and even had children of their own. Clay didn't have a lot in common with them other than baseball. When Johnnie, a 12-year old nephew of one of the principal owners joined the team as a bat boy, Clay befriended him. Johnnie took the role of the kid brother that Clay never had. They were not that different in age. In the locker room and during road games, Clay and the ball boy played video games against each other. The *Madden NFL* was their favorite game, but they also liked *Grand Theft Auto.*

Tragedy struck during a road game scheduled against the Greensboro Grasshoppers, the Florida Marlin's minor league team. It happened during batting practice before the scheduled game. The crowd was just beginning to file in for the game. Clay was written up in the Greensboro paper that day having been interviewed as the future star for the Orioles. Clay was taking batting practice against the pitching coach when he took a mighty swing with his wooden bat. The ball hit the middle of the bat instead of the "sweet spot." The force of Clay's swing resulted in the bat shattering into several large pieces. Johnnie was on the side of the field when it happened. He was retrieving balls that were returning from the outfielders. He wasn't paying attention to Clay's batting. A large piece of Clay's bat went flying into the air towards Johnnie. There was no time for any verbal warning. The fans in the stands were horrified at the sight. The sharp end of the wooden fragment hit Johnnie in the chest penetrating his rib cage. He collapsed onto the field. Blood started seeping out of his wound. At first, everybody froze, not realizing what had happened. Then Clay saw his friend lying on the ground, gasping for air. Seeing this, he jumped out of the batter's box and ran to his friend. The end of the remnant of his bat was still in his hand. He shouted out Johnnie's name. But there was no response. Johnnie was in shock. His eyes rolled towards the back of his head. Clay bent down and held the boy's head into his lap. The momentary silence was broken.

"Help! Somebody call for help!" he cried. This got people into action. The team's trainer who was in the locker room was summoned. An ambulance was called. It came quickly and the driver drove directly onto the field. The boy was lifted into the back of the vehicle drove and it drove away, sirens blasting. Clay was inside the ambulance as it sped to the hospital. The bat fragment pierced Johnnie's heart. He was dying.

"Hang in there buddy. I am sorry. I am so sorry," Clay repeated while sitting off to the side of the gurney. Tears were pouring down his face. The emergency medical technician was trying to control the bleeding as they raced to the ED. But by the time the boy arrived, he had passed. Clay was sitting in the waiting room when the terrible news was confirmed. He just sat there and broke down with grief.

*

Shattered and broken bats that occur after hitting a pitched ball are very common in professional baseball today. However, serious injuries due to flying bat fragments are extremely rare for players and spectators. Late in the 2010 season, Tyler Colvin, a rookie third baseman for the Chicago Cubs was impaled by a broken maple bat on a ball hit by his teammate, Wellington Castillo. Colvin was running down the third base line when it happened. The injured player was sent to a local hospital and recovered without any major incident. It was considered lucky that the bat missile did not puncture his lungs. A shift from bats made out of ash to maple has been cited as a cause for increased breakage from hitting.

In June of 2015, Tonya Carpenter was watching a game between the Oakland As and Boston Red Sox. Oakland's Brett Lawrie hit a ball that fractured his bat. A piece of the bat flew into the stands and struck Tonya's forehead, causing her to bleed profusely. She was immediately evacuated to a Boston hospital with a life threatening injury. Fortunately, Tonya survived. This incident is raising questions about fan security and may result in Major League Baseball instituting new safety precautions.

Major league baseball instituted random drug testing for performance enhancing drugs in the spring of 2006 following various investigations and allegations about many high-profile players. Many

long standing records were broken during baseball's steroid era including
the single season home run records by Mark McGwire and Barry Bonds
and Bond's career records. The policy involves testing during spring
training and random unannounced testing during the season for
performance enhancing drugs and drugs of abuse. Testing for testosterone
and growth hormone was instituted in 2013, including maintaining
records for a player's testosterone and epitestosterone concentrations and
the ratio between the two hormones. Violations of the policy involved
player suspensions and fines that would increase with each violation.
Didehydroepiandrosterone , another naturally occurring anabolic steroid,
was added to the list of banned substances by major league baseball in
2014.

Recently a new test is being investigated for detecting the abuse
of a performance enhancing drug that is also a natural hormone. All
organic compounds are made of the element, carbon. There are two
naturally occurring variants of carbons, called isotopes. The most
common is carbon 12. About 1% of the carbon found in human organic
substances contains the isotope carbon 13. This heavier carbon isotope
can be detected by mass spectrometric instruments used in drug testing.
Pharmaceutical preparations of testosterone have lower $^{13}C/^{12}C$ ratios
and mass spectrometry is increasingly being used to catch cheaters.

Uneven Bars

****

I would characterize myself as a late developer. As a freshman in high school, I only weighed a little over 100 pounds soaking wet. This served me well at first, as I had a choice of joining the wrestling team or gymnastics. I couldn't participate in both sports as they took place concurrently during the winter season. My older brother was a college wrestler at the time I was making this decision. Ok, I know what you are thinking. Wrestling, really? In college, wrestling is a real sport, it is not WWF. But my brother wasn't at the powerhouse Iowa State either, it was M.I.T. He certainly knew his priorities by attending THAT school. I could have been on the varsity wrestling team as a high school freshman in the featherweight category. I competed well against others who were on the team during junior high. In the end, I selected gymnastics and I competed on the team for all four of my high school years. All went well when I first started. I had some experience in junior high and my muscle to body ratio was ideal for the sport. I selected the pommel horse because there was no real chance of me flying off the high bar, trampoline or parallel bars and landing on my head. I was one of the better performers on the freshman team on the side horse; we didn't run vault over the horse like the men and women do now. Over the course of my remaining high school years, my body began filling out, which meant that I was no longer strong enough to be competitive, and my position on the team's side horse depth chart declined. By the time I was a senior, I only got a varsity letter because I stuck the sport out for the entire four years. My only claim to gymnastics greatness was my brief interaction with Bart Connor, the future Gold Medalist of the 1976 in Montreal. Bart grew up in my home town of Morton Grove, Illinois. He was 10 when our coach discovered him, and Bart began working out with us. We knew then he would be great, but I didn't visualize that he would become an international spokesman for the sport. Years later, Bart married Nadia Comaneci of Romania, another member of the international gymnastic royalty and one of the few gymnast who ever got a perfect "10." Thus, it brings me great angst to tell this story....

*

Joanie and Heather lived across the street from each other and were best of friends. It started when they were toddlers. Joanie's mother formed a mother's play group and took the kids to the neighboring park for fun time. It was Joanie's mother that suggested that the two girls enroll into a gymnastic school. Joanie at 5 was a year older and looked out for Heather. During these early years, the girls learned how to do somersaults, cartwheels, and jumps, and nothing that was too difficult. After a year, they progressed to walking and turning on a balance beam. There was no risk for any of the girls getting seriously injured as the 4 inch wide balance beam was only 5 ½ inches off the ground. After a few more years, it was clear that the two girls took to the sport, spending many hours after school at the gym. Joanie and Heather's mothers took turns carpooling them from school to the gym and home. Their coach entered the girls into local meets. Joanie was always the physically stronger competitor. Her routines were filled with power and high-rated athletic skills. Heather was more graceful and elegant than her friend. In those early years, Joanie always beat Heather in their head-to-head competitions. But there was no rivalry, and Heather was happy for Joanie's success.

One day when they were practicing, Joanie developed a rip on the inside of her left hand just below her fingers. A "rip" is when a piece of skin tears off the skin due to excessive friction from doing giant swings on the uneven bars. Men develop rips also from horizontal bar routines. Joanie was sitting in the corner of the gym holding her hand when Heather came by.

Noticing the rip in her hand, Heather remarked, "This happened to me last month and I had to stop for a while."

"What did you use to treat this?" Joanie asked.

"I will ask my mother to give you an aloe plant. The sap from the leaves helped me a lot in soothing the pain," Heather said.

Joanie got the succulent plant and daily rubbed the sap onto her hand. It was a big help and she was appreciative of her friend.

*

The big sad day came when Heather's mother announced that they were moving to another city some 100 miles away. She was a single mom and her employer transferred her to a different location. The two girls, eleven and ten at the time,

161

were devastated, particularly Heather, the younger of the two.

"We'll still see each other at meets," Joanie said trying to comfort her friend. Their level of competition was higher than before. The girls were competing against each other in state and regional competitions. But their loyalty was going to be put to the test in the coming years.

*

Back at the General Hospital, there was an interesting case discussion on precocious puberty during endocrine rounds. My group often participated in these discussions because the field of endocrinology is heavily dependent on the clinical laboratory tests that we provide. We attend to learn about the medical practices and how our hormone, receptor, and antibody assays are used in making decisions. The chief resident, Dr. Dora Resher in the endocrinology service was presenting the case of an 8-year old girl with precocious puberty.

"Our patient is an overweight child who has been menstruating for the past 6 months. She has breast enlargement and auxiliary hair in the pubic region and armpits," Dr. Resher stated. With the child's face covered, the parents gave the resident permission to photograph the child's body in order that doctors in training can learn about this disorder.

"What are the long-term consequences for someone who exhibits early puberty development? Aren't they otherwise normal and healthy? Why should we care?" one of the interns asked.

"These children will likely be short in stature because of the early maturation of their long bones. More importantly, they may have a brain tumor causing an excess release of gonadotropin

162

releasing hormone," Dr. Resher said, as she signaled the radiologist assigned up to the case to the podium from the front row.

"This next slide shows the CT image of her brain. This clearly demonstrates the presence of a tumor in the hypothalamic region." The radiologist illustrated the location of the tumor with his laser pointer.

"If these children go untreated, they will have a much higher risk for breast cancer in adulthood," the chief resident continued. "In this child's case, we were successful in treating her with radiation. But the precocious puberty that resulted from this brain tumor can cause significant psychiatric disease due to teasing from the other children because of their early pubertal development. Therefore, we put this child on a special weight loss diet and a prescription of anastrozole."

One of the interns asked a question. "Wait, did you say anastrozole, the drug used to treat breast cancer?"

"The same medication" the chief resident said. "This drug is an aromatase inhibitor that blocks estrogen production. It is also used off label to treat children with early onset puberty." Everyone in the audience knew that drugs approved by the FDA could be used for other purposes besides the ones advertised by the drug manufacturer. Off label use is at the discretion and responsibility of each doctor. Returning to her slide presentation, Dr. Resher continued. "Here is a photo of our patient today, now 11 years old. As you can see, she has lost a considerable amount of weight, and her breasts have regressed to a more normal size, that is, commensurate with her biological age."

*

Elsewhere in the city, Joanie was wrestling with a decision to use anastrozole. She was now eleven and her body began showing signs of normal maturation. Her hips and thighs grew larger and her breasts began to develop. Both her older sister and mother were full-figured women and she was fearful that she would grow into having the same shape. Most girls in her class welcomed the transformation from a girl to a young woman. But Joanie was obsessed with being a top gymnast with hopes of making the U.S. Olympic team someday. These biological changes were adversely affecting her athletic performance. It first became evident to her after the annual state junior gymnastics championships. For many years, Joanie was the best on the uneven bars for her age group and even for the group above her age. She was also the all-around champion last year, having defeated Heather, her childhood friend. But on this day, Joanie took second to Heather in both the uneven bars and all-around. After the meet, Joanie sat alone in the corner of the gym, still in her uniform and with chalk and tape on her hands. Heather saw her and went to console her friend.

"You just had an off day, Joanie. You'll be back next month," Heather said referring to the upcoming district championship.

Joanie sort of grunted a response but didn't look up. But as Heather started walking away, Joanie jumped up quickly and followed her.

"Hey Heather, would it be okay if I came to your gym one day to watch how you train?" Joanie asked.

"Of course! I would love that. We have sort of grown apart of the years since my family moved, but you know I still love you Joanie. You're the reason I am even in this sport."

Joanie got permission from her parents to take a bus to the city where Heather lived and trained. Heather and her mother picked Joanie up at the bus station and they were off to the gym. They were working out together on each apparatus: the vault, floor exercise, balance beam and then the uneven bars. Joanie could see that Heather had passed her regarding the difficulty rating of the skills she was performing. Heather continued to show that she was graceful and stylish on her floor exercise and balance beam. But with the added height on the vault and release moves on the uneven bars, she was entering a new level of competition.

During the course of that afternoon, Joanie came to the realization that it was her best friend, Heather, who was going to stand in her way to greatness in gymnastics. It was then that she decided to take matters into her own hands. While nobody was looking, Joanie loosened the knob on left side of the upper uneven bars. She then asked Heather to do her latest routine. The coach came by to spot her. All of the other gymnasts in the gym stopped what they were doing to watch. Joanie performed her kip mount on the lower beam and then as she released her grip from that bar, and while flying backwards, grabbed the upper bar with both hands. She did another kip and was about to perform a routine giant swing when the upper bar suddenly slipped down two notches from the weight of her body during the downhill motion. This caused Heather to lose her grip of the bar and she went flying off the apparatus. The accident occurred so quickly and unexpectedly, that her coach, who was spotting her during her routine, did not react in time to catch her or break her fall. Heather landed on the mat directly on her head and neck. She laid there unconscious on the mat. Everybody was horrified and rushed to their fallen teammate. The coach knelt down beside her to make an assessment and told everybody to stand back. The coach quickly saw that this was a serious injury and shouted for someone to call for an ambulance. When help arrived, Heather was still lying where she fell. The paramedics carefully supported her neck in case it was broken and she was rushed to the hospital. Heather's mother was called while at work. She rushed to the hospital where she met Joanie in the waiting area of the emergency room. Joanie said that it was just a freak accident and that she was sure Heather was going to be alright. But deep inside, she was thinking, *mission accomplished.*

*

Heather suffered a sprained neck and was put on neck constraints during her recovery. Her coach withdrew her from the district championship that was to take place the following month. No one ever suspected Joanie's involvement with Heather's accident. With Heather out of the competition, Joanie easily won the un-even bars and balance beam. She took second on the other two events, and won the all-around title. Heather was in the audience cheering on her teammates and her childhood friend.

Back home with medals in hand, Joanie contemplated her next move. She needed to somehow slow down her rate of puberty. She went on the internet and learned about drugs used to treat precocious puberty. When she scanned the list of medications, she recognized one in particular. Her grandmother suffered from breast cancer and Joanie remembered that her mother told her that she was being treated with anastrozole. Grandma lived in a house nearby and Joanie was very close to her. Grandma purchased the medication through the mail from a Canadian company. She later switched to tamoxifen because it was cheaper and stopped ordering online. Without telling her mother or grandmother, Joanie found the old prescription records and she began refilling her grandmother's order through the mail by forging her signature. She opened up a post office box, and told the drug company that the recipient moved to a new address. Joanie sent money orders through the mail to pay for these shipments. Soon, Joanie was taking the puberty arresting drug. Not only did the drug inhibit release of hormones, but within a few months, her body began to regress to her pre-pubescent state. Her muscle-to-fat ratio increased and soon she was performing her gymnastic routines better than ever. Joanie's mother noticed that her youngest daughter was shorter than her older sister when she was at that age, but concluded that she was just a late bloomer. With Heather out of action, Joanie was winning most of the junior events. The coaches began talking about her potential to win the adult events and at 14, competing for a national championship.

In the meantime, quietly Heather continued her rehabilitation and return to the sport. Joanie stopped calling Heather and the two grew apart. Heather re-appeared during the regional championship. She was second in the all-around to Joanie, but the people closest to the sport could see that Heather might be strong competition for Joanie and the other gymnasts vying for a slot on the Olympic team.

Joanie believed she needed to act against Heather again

in order to achieve her goals in the sport. She reasoned that a second "accident" while Joanie was in the gym would arouse suspicion. Therefore, a more extreme plan was necessary. Joanie was dating an older high school boy named Roberto, who adored Joanie. He told her that he would do anything to help her succeed. Joanie asked Roberto to assault Heather to the point that she could not compete at the national championships. Roberto went to Heather's school and followed her home one day. When they were alone, he ran up to her from behind and struck her on her left elbow with a small wooden baseball bat fracturing the condylar bone. Heather fell to the ground screaming in pain while her assailant fled the scene. With her good arm, she called her mother for help. She was taken to the emergency department for the second time in four years.

Heather's injury ended her gymnastics career. While the bone healed, it was not as strong as before and she had difficulty gripping the uneven bars. No one linked Joanie or Roberto to the heinous act they perpetrated on Heather. Joanie competed in the national championship but did not qualify for either the Olympic team or as an alternate in any of the events. In retrospect, her attack on Heather did not affect the outcome of her bid to qualify for the Games. A few months later, Joanie's mother found anastrozol pills in her daughter's closet and confronted her. Joanie confessed to taking the pills to retard her puberty. Her mother admitted her daughter to a psychiatric unit and destroyed the remaining pills. Within a few years, Joanie grew to adult size and she was no longer able to compete in gymnastics. Her final height at 5'1" proved to be much shorter than either her sister or mother. She was also much heavier. In her ambition to excel in gymnastics, Joanie made decisions that stunted her growth and had a life-long effect on her psyche.

*

This fictitious story is similar to the real events that occurred in the U.S. and International ice skating world. In 1994, Tonya Harding and Nancy Kerrigan were American figure skaters competing against each other during the U.S. National Figure Skating Championships. Harding's ex-husband hired a man to assault Kerrigan so that she could not compete against Harding at the championship. The man struck Kerrigan on her right leg with a police baton, forcing her out of the National Championship. Both Kerrigan and Harding competed in the 1994 Olympics in Lillehammer, Norway, taking second and eight, respectively. Harding acknowledged knowing about the attack and pleaded guilty to conspiring to hinder prosecution of the attackers. She was banned from any further events by the U.S. Figure Skating Association and received no invitations to join any of the professional skating tours.

Puberty-delaying medications are not specifically tested by the Olympic committee. Therefore the incidence of this abuse is unknown. Anastrozol is banned by the Olympic committee but in the arena of weight lifters, it is used to counter the estrogenic side effects of anabolic steroid abuse.

So what became of some of the seniors on the 1971 Niles West High School gymnastics team in Skokie Illinois? We did not distinguish ourselves in the world of gymnastics like Bart Conner. But our all-around performer during those years, Robert Kushner, M.D., is a Professor of Medicine, -General Internal Medicine and Geriatrics at the Northwestern University Comprehensive Center on Obesity and author of Counseling Overweight Adults: The Lifestyle Patterns Approach and Toolkit, the American Medical Association's Assessment and Management of Obesity, Dr. Kushner's Personality Type Diet, Treatment of the Obese Patient and Fitness Unleashed: A Dog and Owner's Guide to Losing Weight and Gaining Health.   *Ben Jaremus, my compadre on the side horse, retired as a paramedic and former Chief of the Evanston, Illinois Fire Department. After his retirement, he saved the life of a man in Mount Prospect Illinois, by performing emergency CPR on someone who stopped breathing. Thomas Abshire, M.D. who was a specialist on the trampoline and parallel bars, went to the US Air Force Academy in Colorado Springs after high school and is the Senior Vice President of the Blood Center of Wisconsin and Professor of Pediatrics and Medicine at the Medical College of Wisconsin. And I didn't do too badly professionally, considering my gymnastics career was a bust. The NCAA runs an ad regarding student athletes stating that the majority are "going Pro in something other than sports." Maybe it was the discipline of being a gymnast that enabled many of us to strive for perfection.*

Too Tall for Comfort

****

Frankie Carter was the third of 7 total siblings in her family. She and her brothers and sisters towered over the other kids in her class. It ran in the family because both of her parents were over six feet, and Regina, the mother, had an Uncle that played professional basketball. But because Frankie was different, she was the victim of torment by the other children. They called her "sky scraper", "beanstalk", a "tall drink of water", and "lanky Franky." As a result, she had few friends and was introverted. She rarely spoke up in class and hated standing in front of the class to speak or write something on the blackboard. Frankie was also nearsighted and wore classes at an early age. This led to further teasing by her classmates. Things got better when she got prescription contact lenses.

During the late 1960s, there weren't many sports for high school girls. There was little prospect for any college scholarships for her, and only a handful of women were successful in professional women sports. Frankie grew up before there was Title IX, a portion of the U.S. Education Amendment, which passed in 1972, that mandated equal opportunity for women as well as men in educational programs and activities sponsored by the federal government. Frankie's time in high school was also before Billie Jean King's famous 'Battle of the Sexes" match between her and Bobby Riggs in 1973. Billie Jean won the match propelling professional women's tennis to the standing it has today.

Frankie was fortunate that she was born in Southern California. There, she played beach volleyball, which at the time was in its infancy. She started at a young age and her height was a big advantage. Frankie was 6 feet 6 inches tall by the time she was a senior. She and her older sister played doubles at Manhattan Beach. They won many beach tournaments even as juniors and against male players.

Frankie was recruited by Houston State University and received the first full athletic scholarship offered to a woman. This was despite the fact that she had never played organized volleyball indoors before. On the beach, there are just two players who have to do everything: serve, dig, set, block, spike and dink. Indoors, there are six players with a specialization of positions. The "middle blockers" are usually the tallest players who can block middle hits without having to jump high. The "setters" have to have good hands and be quick on their feet to get to the balls. The "liberos" are back row specialists that dig out spikes, dive for balls, and retrieve errant passes. The outside hitters were usually the best athletes and often the stars of the team. They would get the high sets at the edge of the court near the sideline. Frankie was the tallest woman on the team. She also had unusually long arms and fingers and thus was a natural middle hitter and blocker. She could jump very high and reach over the net with her arms to block balls just after the spiker on the other team hit it.

Frankie's coach at HSU was Toji, a former Olympian from the Japanese National Team. He was relentless with Frankie. He drilled her harder than any of the other players. There was one practice during the first week of her college career that set the tone for the coach/player relationship. During a digging drill, each player, one by one had their hands together out in front with bent knees and Toji was spiking balls at them. Then he would throw another ball about 6 feet off to one side, requiring the player to dive or roll to bump the ball, then the next player entered the fray. It was a routine drill that all volleyball players engage in during practice. But on this day, Toji, who was always very accurate with his spikes during the drill, hit a ball especially hard and directly at Frankie's head. She didn't react fast enough and the ball hit squarely into his star freshman's face. She fell backwards and was stunned. The hit rattled her vision and she had difficulty focusing for a few minutes. Little did she or her coach know that the lens in Frankie's left eye shifted upon impact.

Toji said, "Get up Frankie. You have to be prepared for any spike." Most of the other players were stunned by this but they didn't say anything. The more senior players on the team knew that Coach Toji hit her on purpose to send a message that this was his team and nobody was a star.

After practice, one of Frankie's teammates asked, "How come you don't complain about being treated more harshly than the other girls?"

"Coach is just trying to make me better. I need to be prepared for anything he dishes out." Frankie was right. It ultimately made her a better player, which was Toji's main

173

objective.

Frankie was the starting middle blocker for the varsity team in her freshman year. There was a buzz on the campus for Frankie as a black female athlete starting in her first game. Women's sports were not as popular as they are today, but Frankie owned the audience on this night. The team easily defeated their rival, Houston Baptist University.

*

A few months later, about a thousand miles away, another volleyball player entered his first college game, substituting in the back row for his team's star player. This event did not entail any of the fanfare or notoriety that Frankie's debut caused. This player was 9 inches shorter than Frankie, and played on a men's volleyball net, which was 7-½ inches higher. He was also Asian. I was a sophomore the first year that I played competitive volleyball. By my senior year, I was the starting setter for the Purdue University volleyball team. This was an interscholastic "club sport" which simply meant that there was little sponsorship for travel, equipment, or uniforms. But we still played against full varsity college teams. The powerhouse teams then were Ohio State University coached by Doug Beal, currently the CEO of Volleyball USA, and Ball State University coached by Don Shondell, whose team won the first NCAA Men's volleyball championship in 1970. The next year I was one of the starting setters, and by my senior year, 1975, I was selected to be on the second team of the Midwest Intercollegiate Volleyball Association. Even with this success, I knew there was no professional volleyball playing or big time coaching job in my future. I went on to graduate school instead and became a professional in an arena other than sports

*

As a middle hitter/blocker, Frankie got sets that were short in height, which did not allow the defense enough time to mount two players to block her. When she got the set, it almost always resulted in a kill or a point for her side. Many times, however, the bump to the setter was too far from the middle of the court and the middle hitter was not able to get the set. Thus, Frankie didn't get as many kills as the team and Toji wanted. After a successful freshman year, Toji moved Frankie from middle blocker to outside hitter so that she would be available for more sets. The other team also knew about her power and strength, and often countered with a triple block rather than the customary two-man variety. At first, this defensive strategy did not work because Frankie tried to hit through the hands of the blockers but the ball would come back to her side. Toji then taught her how to hit "high," so that her spike would go over the shorter blockers, and still land in the court at a high rate of speed, and into the empty space behind the blockers where none of the diggers were positioned. She also learned how to "tool" players, spiking the ball off the blockers with such speed, that it would land far out of bounds. Tooling is not as effective strategy to a middle hitter because these shots off the block could be retrieved by the defense. When Frankie perfected both shots, she was unstoppable in the front row. Soon, she also became proficient at winning points from "back row" hits as well. These are sets that are 10 feet away from the net, instead of the normal sets that are 1-2 feet away.

Frankie played for three years and then left the team and

college. Houston State finished second in the country in each of her last two years. Frankie left college with one year of eligibility remaining to join the USA National Women's Volleyball team. When ask why she didn't stay one more year to get her degree she said, "I can always go back to school when my volleyball career is over. But for now, I have an opportunity to help our National team. Who knows how long I can play at the top level? My health might not last forever."

*

At Mount Sinai in New York, Dr. Russell Thomas was a pediatrician and researcher. His specialty was treating children suffering from a genetic disease affecting their connective tissue. These children were usually tall with long limbs, fingers, and toes. They may also have abnormalities in the lenses of their eyes causing poor vision and astigmatism. The syndrome was first described in 1896 after a French pediatrician. Many of these children died very young due to defects in their cardiac valves and aorta. Based on an analysis of families, it was known that this disease was autosomal dominate; if one parent had the disease, the chances of a child getting it was 50%. In 1991, Dr. Russell and his colleagues discovered a mutation in the gene that encodes fibrillin-1, a protein that is part of the elastic fibers of connective tissue. As the name suggests, connective tissue serves to hold organs into their rightful place like scaffolding does in the construction of a building. Connective tissue is found throughout the body. A defect in the protein causes the abnormal production of the scaffolding. The building that is produced in this way is weak and vulnerable.

*

The US National Volleyball Team couldn't wait until Frankie joined their ranks. Overnight, their team went from being marginal to a world contender. Frankie played on the team for eight years and qualified for two Olympic Games. The 1980 Moscow games, however, were boycotted by President Carter, and the US volleyball teams stayed home. In 1984, the games were held in Los Angeles. Frankie was inspired playing in front of her home town, and the National team won the Silver Medal.

Frankie dated John Hurley, a middle hitter from the men's national volleyball team that won the Gold medal at the LA games. Because Frankie was so tall, she didn't have a lot of options when it came to men. Most of the professional basketball players were too arrogant for her taste. John was a few inches taller than Frankie and had the temperament she was looking for. At first, he helped her with her volleyball skills.

"At this level, you have to train yourself to see at where the blockers are while you are hitting the ball," he told her. "They are as tall as you are and they can jump just as high, so you cannot just spike over the blockers like you did in college." This was the hardest part of international volleyball. You have to train your eyes to focus on the ball and the opponents at the same time, while in the middle of your jump, and adjust your swing at the ball accordingly.

Frankie appreciated the instruction. It didn't hurt that John was good muscular and good looking too. Soon, they were spending a lot of their free time together, working on weights and running. Then it was dinner and a movie. It wasn't long before he fell in love with her, and one day, he proposed.

"Just think, between you and me, our children will be

super athletes," he said.

"I love you John, you know that, but I have more to do in volleyball. We have plenty of time to be together to grow old and have kids after our knee pads are used up." Frankie was referring to the equipment they wore as players.

After the 1984 Olympics, Frankie got an offer to play professional volleyball in Europe. John developed recurrent shoulder problems and planned to retire from the sport after the Games. He was accepted into medical school in Texas and would be starting classes in the fall. Frankie went on to join an Italian team. The couple kept in constant communication and visited each other whenever possible. They planned on getting married after John finished school and before he started his residency.

Then one day, during practice, Frankie was in a digging line. The coach was spiking balls at her just like Toji did some 15 years earlier. After a strenuous practice, Frankie and the other players sat on the floor along the sideline of the court with a towel over her shoulder. She slowly rolled onto her side and closed her eyes. She was thinking of what John was doing. At that very moment, John was in the first year anatomy class with his hands inside a cadaver. He and his medical student partner had excised the heart and John had it in his hands. But his mind was half way around the world. He was thinking of Frankie. The coach came over to the women.

"Everybody get up. Spiking drills," he said with a distinct Italian accent.

Each player arose and slowly walked towards the middle of the court where the coach was standing. Frankie remained on the floor. "You too Frankie," the coach said. But Frankie did not move. "Are you ok?" he asked. He shook her but got no response. "Somebody call the team doctor, right away." But it was no use, Frankie was dead.

*

Forty years after my college career ended, I am still playing competitive volleyball in the form of senior games. Having lost most of the height off my vertical jump really puts me at a competitive disadvantage against taller players who don't have to jump as high to spike and block. But I am faster than most and this serves me well in setting and playing defense.

*

This story is based on the life and career of Flo Hyman who died of Marfan's syndrome 1986. This is not a tale about performance enhancing drugs, as she was naturally talented, and physically predisposed to excel in the sport of volleyball (tall and having long arms). In this story, a mutant gene was the "Hidden Assassin." Marfan's syndrome was named after the French pediatrician who first described the condition in a paper published in 1896. The syndrome is characterized by changes in the skeletal system resulting in most victims being tall and having disproportionately long and slender limbs, fingers, and toes. There can also be changes to the lenses of the eyes resulting in nearsightedness and astigmatism. The incidence of Marfan's syndrome is about 1 in 5,000. Hyman was not diagnosed with Marfan's syndrome while she was alive, but in retrospect, she had the physical appearance of someone who was afflicted by this disease. Her autopsy showed that Hyman had an aortic dissection, a tear in the large vessel carrying oxygenated blood away from the heart and to the rest of her body.

Marfan's syndrome is an autosomal dominant genetic disease, therefore it affects both men and women equally. In 1991, five years after the death of Flo Hyman, Dr. Francesco Ramirez at Mount Sinai Medical Center in New York linked the disease to a mutation in the gene that produces fibrillin-1. This is an essential protein that forms the elastic fibers in connective tissue. A defective fibrillin protein also blocks its binding to transforming growth factor beta (TGF-β), an important cell signaling factor needed for normal structure and function of vascular smooth muscle. Since his initial publication, there have been thousands of different mutations that have been reported in the literature. Many cases of Marfan's syndrome are caused by a point mutation, i.e., the substitution of one nucleic acid base for another. A change in the "blueprint" for fibrillin causes a different amino acid to be incorporated into the protein itself. A substituted amino acid in a key location can cause the protein to fold differently resulting in its malfunction. Not all causes of Marfan's syndrome are inherited. About a quarter of cases are not transmitted through a parent, but occur through a spontaneous mutation. In an individual suspected of Marfan's syndrome, the diagnosis is confirmed by the clinical lab with the detection of a genetic variance in the fibrillin-1 gene sequence. The syndrome can be effectively treated with cardiac medications that can reduce TGF-β levels, regulate blood pressure, reduce the heart rate, and when used in children with Marfan's syndrome, reduce the rate of aortic aneurysms.

With therapeutics and lifestyle precautions, individuals with Marfan's syndrome can have a normal lifespan. In 2014, Isaiah Austin was a 7 foot 1 inch star center for the Baylor basketball team. Five days before the NBA draft, he was diagnosed with Marfan's syndrome. Under the advice of his doctors, Austin gave up his dream to become a professional athlete.

Because of his height and physical appearance, President Abraham Lincoln was once thought to have Marfan's syndrome. In

1991, a group of geneticists debated about testing Lincoln's DNA from samples of his blood and tissue that exists within national archives. An important issue was Lincoln's family rights to privacy. In the end, the committee decided not to do testing because of the growing number of mutations that were being discovered each year. Today, it would be possible to sequence Lincoln's fibrillin gene to determine if he suffered from the disease. However from the President's autopsy records, since there was no reported evidence of abnormalities in his aorta or the lenses in his eyes. This has led many scientists in recent years, to discount the theory that Lincoln had Marfan's syndrome.

Crescentoid Blood

We received blood from an ER doctor in Denver from Jewanna White, a 17-year old patient. It was sent to us because we offered a specialized assay for hemoglobin based on liquid chromatography. It was our policy to first test the sample using a standard hemoglobin electrophoresis, a test widely used in most hospital laboratories. If there were any unusual hemoglobin species present, we then used the specialized assay to determine the identity of the variant. After the electrophoresis, my tech came to show me the result.

"I don't understand," Cynthia said. Electrophoresis is a technique used to separate proteins present in blood. "Both our agarose and cellulose acetate gels confirm hemoglobin A and S. So there was nothing unusual here to warrant using our special test." Her confusion was that we see dozens of patterns just like this from other patients every week. Using a combination of gels, there are no other hemoglobin variants that appear in this manner. "What's even more confusing is that the doctor ordered this test as STAT."

Circulating red blood cells contain hemoglobin, an important protein that transports oxygen from the lungs to tissues and organs. While most individuals have hemoglobin "A," there are many genetic variants. An individual who has two copies of the hemoglobin S variant has sickle cell disease. These individuals have reduced ability to deliver oxygen. Instead of being round and doughnut shaped, sickle red blood cells are elongated, crescent-like shapes that are fragile which leads to breakdown. They are also sticky which can cause a stroke by the accumulation of cells at arterial branching points. I confirmed Cynthia's finding that this patient was a sickle cell carrier. My tech was puzzled because this variant is readily detectable and does not require use of our specialized procedure.

"Hemoglobin testing is not on our STAT list," I told Cynthia, "but some doctors order everything as STAT. What is more interesting is why they sent this sample to us for confirmation, since the result is straightforward. I need to do some investigation..."

*

Jewanna and her older sister Nakeisha grew up in Northern California. Their interest in tennis began when Venus and Serena Williams played each other in the 2000 Wimbledon semifinals. Venus beat her younger sister that day, and went on to win the Championship.

"Let's take up tennis," Nakeisha said to her sister. "We could be the next Williams sisters." The girls were 7 and 9 years old at the time.

"I don't understand the rules. Why is the first point called '15' and the second point '30?" Jewanna asked.

"Don't worry Jewanna. I will teach you the rules."

For the next several years, Jewanna and Nakeisha spent many hours on tennis courts at a public park near their home.

They were both natural athletes with good hand-eye coordination. Nakeisha was the stronger of the two while Jewanna was fast on her feet. Their game improved when they signed up for group clinics offered by the park district. Soon, they were entering junior tennis tournaments, playing both singles, and teamed up together for doubles. Nakeisha in particular wanted to be a professional tennis player. Jewanna was not as ambitious, and was happy to play with her sister.

That all came to an abrupt end one summer evening. Jewanna and Nakeisha had just completed a workout on the court and were going home on their bicycles.

"You go on ahead, I want to work on my serve," Nakeisha told her younger sister. Jewanna was nursing a sore elbow and wanted to leave. "See you at dinner" Jewanna said as she got on her bicycle and headed home. After hitting 50 serves, Nakeisha picked up the balls, stuffed them into her backpack alongside her racket, and got on her bike. While riding, she was thinking about how she needed a "kick" second serve, when it happened. A businessman who had too much to drink was on his way to another bar. He came upon Nakeisha but didn't notice her. Just as he was passing her, his arm made an involuntary twitch and the car swerved. The front of the car hit the young girl who flew off the bike. Her head hit the pavement and she began bleeding. Nakeisha was not wearing a helmet. The man stopped the car and rushed out to see what happened. He saw the crushed bicycle and a young girl lying face down. A bystander called for an ambulance. When it arrived, the paramedics loaded the injured girl onto their stretcher and rushed her to the local hospital. Nakeisha suffered a traumatic brain injury and died of her injuries 36 hours later.

Her death devastated Jewanna. She went into a deep depression. Jewanna rarely got out of bed and didn't go outside for several weeks. Her parents tried to comfort her but it was no use, as she had lost her best friend. Just before school was to start, Nakeisha visited Jewanna in a dream.

"Jewanna, you must get yourself together. It is time to get over your grief. You have to live for the both of us now. We started something in tennis. It is up to you to take over. I know you can do this. I am in a good place so don't worry about me. Someday we will be together again. But for now, there is much for you to do. Get up! Get going! Don't disappoint me."

The next day, Jewanna woke up with an entirely new attitude. She wasn't sure if she dreamt last night about Nakeisha or if Nakeisha actually had come to her bed. It didn't matter anymore. Jewanna was given a resolve from her sister and she was determined to make her sister proud of her. For the next several years, Jewanna devoted herself to her school studies and tennis. She made the varsity team as a freshman and was the number one singles player during her sophomore year and beyond. She refused to play doubles, reserving her memory of her and Nakeisha playing. Nakeisha received an athletic scholarship to play tennis at Cal State, Richmond.

The CSU Richmond coach was Gabriel Lopez, a former tennis standout at the school. Gabriel spent a few years on the Professional Tour but never reached a ranking below 300. A knee injury when he was 30 ended his pro career. Gabriel returned to CSU to coach both the men's and women's tennis teams. He took a particular liking to Jewanna, because like himself, she had learned the game through public park programs and not from country club lessons. Jewanna and the other freshmen recruits came to Gabriel's office for an orientation.

"Our school requires a physical examination and routine blood testing before athletes can participate. The NCAA has a policy of random urine drug testing. They will be looking for the presence of recreational and performance enhancing drugs. I have no tolerance for drugs. If they find you positive, you will lose your scholarship. I know none of you are on any 'juice.' I don't think it really helps tennis players anyway, as this is a game of skill. We will also test each of you for sickle cell disease or trait. While this is highly unlikely for most of you, it can occur in some ethnic minorities." Gabriel was looking straight at Jewanna as he was speaking. She didn't know much about sickle cell disease, but was sure it didn't apply to her. "You will be notified when it is time to undergo these tests. In the meantime, start working out. Practice begins on Monday. Our first match is in 6 weeks against Denver State. They're good so we'll have to be on top of our game."

*

Jewanna's physical exam was scheduled a few weeks later. The weather was extremely warm and dry the week before. She drank a lot of water to keep hydrated. Jewanna had a series of nose bleeds due to the arid conditions. To make matters worse, she also had her period. Jewanna suffered severe cramps and unusually heavy blood flow. She missed classes and practice on the heaviest of the days.

The physical was conducted by Dr. Livingstone, the team's doctor. Jewanna had normal blood pressure, her heart rate was low, which was typical for highly conditioned athletes, and there were no abnormalities noted following her eyes, ears, and throat exam. Blood was collected for routine lab work. The doctor also explained to Jewanna the blood test for sickle cell disease. When the lab tests came back a few days later, Dr. Livingstone noted a few abnormal results. He asked Jewanna to see him.

"Jewanna, how are you feeling? Are you tired?"

"I feel fine doctor," was Jewanna's response.

"Are you menstruating regularly?" Dr. Livingstone asked. From his experience, many female athletes have irregular menstrual cycles due the extensive exercise.

"Yes, every month like clockwork. Why is that important," Jewanna responded.

"During your period, do you bleed a lot?"

"Yes from time to time. Last month's period was pretty heavy."

Dr. Livingstone was recording Jewanna's responses into her medical records. "Do you take vitamins?"

"No. What did the lab find?" Jewanna was getting a little worried about these questions.

"Your red blood cell count and serum iron value are low," the doctor said. "You have iron-deficiency anemia. It is not a major concern. I am going to put you on iron supplements. This will help keep you healthy and improve your stamina while on the tennis court.

"Ok doctor. I'll do whatever it takes." She was about to leave the office when she remembered.

"Oh, what about the results of my sickle cell test?"

Jewanna asked.

"It came out negative. You don't have sickle cell disease or the trait. You are cleared to play. Good luck on your season. I expect great things from you and your team."

"Thanks doctor," Jewanna left the office with a sigh of relief. She could now concentrate on getting ready for Denver State.

*

Jewanna was the best player on the Cal State Richmond's women's tennis team. Coach Lopez put her into the number two slot so that there wouldn't be any pressure on her to succeed in her first college match. Jewanna didn't mind, she was just eager to play. The team took a flight to Denver and arrived the day before the match. Ideally, they should have come a few days before the match so that the athletes could get acclimated to the high altitude conditions of Colorado. But in college sports, there is no time or money for sending players in advance. While it was early September, Denver was experiencing an Indian summer. It was very hot and humid. Coach Lopez reminded his players to drink a lot of water.

Jewanna's opponent was someone who had the same tennis style as she. Both were baseline players. They covered their side of the court extremely well with their speed and came to the net only when absolutely necessary. Neither of them had big serves and so there were no aces or quick points. Because of this, the rallies were very long and tiring to both players. Jewanna's match was in the middle of the second set when all of the other matches were over. Because each school split the other matches, the winner of Jewanna's match would decide the team winner.

Jewanna lost the first set and faced match point several times during the second set, but she was able to win the critical point. The second set came down to a tie breaker, which Jewanna won 7 points to 5. The women took a short break before starting the third and decisive set. Jewanna was very tired and breathing heavily. Gabriel asked her if she was able to continue.

"I feel fine Coach. I can beat her. I won't let the team down." Gabriel kept her in the match. Jewanna could sense that somewhere above her, Nakeisha was pushing her on to win. The third set was as grueling as the first two. The match time was approaching two hours. Both competitors were exhausted and playing on the natural adrenaline from their bodies. The score was 5-4 and Jewanna was serving for the match. Normally, the server would have an edge, but both players had their serves broken on several occasions. It was not a given that Jewanna would win. She sat in her chair between the changeover. The other were routing her on.

"You can do it Jewanna! One more game." The girls from the other team were doing the same for their teammate.

Coach Lopez made a comment to the team's student trainer. "This is what college sports are all about."

Jewanna wiped the perspiration off her brow, took a drink of water, grabbed her racket, and headed towards her side of the court. Then she appeared to trip and fell forward. The racket flew out of her hands. She braced herself for the fall. While on the hot asphalt court, she groaned. Then it became dark. Her eyes were closed and she did not get up. Everyone from both sides was stunned and motionless. Coach Lopez and the trainer ran to her. She lay unconscious.

In the emergency room, Jewanna's core temperature was 102 °F. Her clothes were removed and ice packs were placed around her body to cool her down. Jewanna was severely dehydrated and was given intravenous fluids. When blood tests showed that she had a low hemoglobin and hematocrit count, the blood was cross-matched and typed, and two units of packed red blood cells were administered. She also had a very high activity of creatine kinase, an enzyme that is released from skeletal muscles. Within a few hours, her kidneys shut down from release of myoglobin, another protein of muscles. She was treated with sodium bicarbonate to alkalinize her urine and diuretics to improve her circulation by removing fluid. A peripheral red blood smear showed the presence of sickle cells. An order was placed for hemoglobin electrophoresis. The lab was called and asked to perform the test STAT. The pathologist in charge of the lab came to the emergency department stating that the patient was a carrier for the sickle cell trait. In the waiting room, Dr. Brooks, the ER doc met with Coach Lopez and the trainer.

"Coach, Jewanna is suffering from a sickle cell crisis," Dr. Brooks said. "Our lab has determined that she has the sickle cell trait. Coach Lopez, did you know that she was a carrier?"

"Doctor, according to NCAA regulations, our athletes are all tested. I reviewed the reports on all of our incoming players and distinctly remembered that Jewanna's result was negative. I would have pulled her from playing singles had I known she had this disease trait."

"We'll have to check all of the records. There is a remote possibility that our lab might have it wrong. I know an investigator who has a specialized procedure for confirming hemoglobinopathies. We'll collect a fresh blood sample and send it to his lab for testing right away. In the meantime, we are doing all that we can to save her life. She is being admitted to the intensive care unit."

Coach Lopez returned to his team at the hotel and gathered the players in the lobby in a circle. They said a prayer for Jewanna's recovery. The coach suggested that they go to dinner together, but none of them were hungry. They sat in the lobby holding hands. Most of the girls were crying. Coach Lopez was called back to the hospital the next day. There he was given word that Jewanna had passed that evening. She never regained consciousness. Her body was shipped home where she was buried next to her sister.

*

The university conducted an investigation as to the circumstances surrounding Jewanna's death. Coach Lopez was temporarily relieved of his coaching duties pending the outcome of the investigation. The tennis team postponed all of their matches until further notice.

I was asked to opine on the discrepancy between the screening test for sickle cell disease, the electrophoresis method conducted at the Denver hospital, and our confirmatory procedure. In formulating my opinion, I reviewed Jewanna's medical records. After careful review, I deliberated my findings to the committee.

"I believe the sickle cell screening test produced a falsely negative result. Our results and those of the hospital in Denver confirmed that Jewanna had sickle cell trait. I have also obtained records from the California Newborn Screening Laboratory.

Their records show that she was a sickle cell carrier. My conclusion is that the sickle cell screening test that was sent to a lab by the University produced an erroneous result," I paused a few moments waiting for an anticipated question.

A member of the committee asked, "How could this have happened? Are the testing procedures different?"

"Yes, the screening test involves lysing red cells to free the hemoglobin protein into solution. Hemoglobin is reduced by the dithionite reagent. The normal reduced hemoglobin A is soluble. Hemoglobin S is insoluble. The test involves holding the tube in front of a piece of paper containing a black line. If the line can be seen through the tube, the result is negative. If the line is not visible, the result is positive, indicating hemoglobin S."

One of the committee members was flabbergasted. "Are you kidding? With all of the sophisticated equipment you have in the laboratory today, this is the best you can do? This poor girl's life was dependent on a manual visual test!?"

"Unfortunately, yes. That is why we don't use this method. But it is a test that has been used for decades because it is very inexpensive and there aren't many cases of false negative results."

"Is this what happened here?" was his next question.

"From her lab records, Jewanna was very anemic at the time blood was collected for her sickle cell test. Anemia is a recognized cause of a false negative result by the Sickledex test" referring to the commercial name of the test used. "I have the package insert here that states that a hemoglobin level of less than 7 can cause a false negative. Jewanna's hemoglobin count was

7.9. Jewanna reported losing a lot of blood during her menstrual period. Her roommate mentioned that she was also prone to nose bleeds. She also drank a lot of water which further diluted her red cell volume. I don't think anybody is at fault here. Maybe your doctor should have known about this limitation, but few doctors know about the limitation of any clinical lab test. You will have to determine if the coach exercised poor judgment in letting his athlete play, but there was no reason for him to know that she was genetically predisposed to harm."

After a few more questions, the Committee adjourned. They did not hold Coach Lopez responsible and he was reinstated. The findings were reported to Jewanna's family. They were satisfied that the investigation was conducted properly and to their credit, they did not initiate a lawsuit. A plaque was placed over one of the 10 tennis courts at California State University Richmond. It was engraved with: "The Jewanna White Tennis Court at CSU Richmond."

*

Sickle cell disease affects people living or originating from sub-Saharan Africa, the West Indies, and South Asia. It is caused by a mutation in the gene for hemoglobin where the amino acid valine is inserted instead of glutamic acid. An individual who inherits two copies of the defective gene has sickle cell disease, while someone with the trait has only one copy. The incidence of sickle cell disease is in the U.S. is 1 in 500 African Americans. Approximately 1 in 12 individuals are sickle cell carriers.

This is a fictitious story. To date, there have been no NCAA athletes with sickle cell trait who have died on the field of play. There have, however, been college football players who have passed following workouts. In 2006, Dale Lloyd was a football player on the Rice University team and he had sickle cell trait. After a strenuous workout on a hot day in Texas, he collapsed on the field and died the next day due to rhabdomyolysis, a condition characterized by a total breakdown of the individual's skeletal muscle. Lloyd's family settled a wrongful death lawsuit against Rice University, the NCAA, the coach, and school doctors. In 2010, the NCAA decided that all incoming Division I student-athletes must be either tested for the sickle cell trait, show proof that a prior test was conducted, or sign a waiver releasing the institution from liability if they decline.

High altitude is a risk factor for subjects with sickle cell trait. The oxygen content at sea level is 20.9%. In Denver, the 'Mile High' city, the content is less than 17.2%. Ryan Clark was a safety for the Pittsburgh Steelers and suffered a sickle cell crisis following an away game against the Denver Broncos in 2007. His crisis required surgery to remove both his spleen and gallbladder. Four years later, he sat out an important playoff game against the Broncos in Denver because of his sickle cell trait. The Steelers lost that game.

The California Newborn Screening Laboratory instituted mandatory testing in 1990 for sickle cell disease for all children born in the state. I have been the medical director at this lab for the past few years. The testing laboratories under our jurisdiction do not use the sickle cell solubility test. As a result, I believe the rate of false negative results today is zero.

To ECG or Not To ECG

The debate was organized by Willard Link, a family practice physician. Dr. Link was the vice president of the Association for Family Practice Physicians and Program Chair for their annual meeting held at the Moscone Center in San Francisco. I don't normally attend this meeting but for scientific and medical reasons, I was particularly drawn to one of the scheduled debates. The principal question was, "Should we screen competitive athlete's risk for sudden cardiac death through the use of the electrocardiogram?" I attended because I am a "weekend athlete" and have performed extensive research in cardiovascular disease. On the "Pro" side was Dr. Alan Mader of the University of California, San Diego. On the "Con" side was Dr. Robert Prolis of Columbia University. Dr. Link was the moderator for the session. There were over 500 people in attendance. Each doctor got 20 minutes. This was followed by a 40 minute discussion including questions from the audience. Members of the local "medical media" were also on hand to report the proceedings.

Dr. Mader was first to speak. "According to the NCAA, sudden cardiac death in young subjects has an incidence of 1 in 44 thousand athletes between the ages of 17 and 23 years old. The most common cause is hypertrophic cardiomyopathy." I knew that this was a form heart failure that begins very early in life. "Like other forms of cardiomyopathy, this one is characterized by an enlargement of the heart. This disease is often asymptomatic. There have been many cases of sudden death in athletes during or immediately after an athletic event. We know that stress can release adrenaline which can be toxic to a heart that is predisposed to problems. The immediate cause of death is a cardiac arrhythmia. We can detect who might have hypertrophic cardiomyopathy by finding an abnormal heart rhythm through an electrocardiogram." The science and medical reporters were busy taking notes.

"It only takes a few minutes and it has the potential to save countless lives." This latter statement was made for the benefit of the media covering the debate.

"ECG screening is mandated by law among competitive athletes in Italy. Their program demonstrated a reduction in deaths from 3.6 per 100,000 before implementation of the screening program to 0.4 per 100,000 some 20 years later. I believe we owe it to our children playing sports that we screen them for risks due to abnormal heart function before they engage in the activity."

*

He and his friend Bo transformed the sports scene at this university near the Los Angeles Airport. They were first recruited to play on the University of Southern California basketball team but their freshman season was a bust and the athletic department fired the coach and assistant coach. Bo, his friend and other teammates wanted input as to who would be the next Trojan's coach. Instead, the new coach was hired without any of their advice and there was some dissension among the returning players, he gave the players an ultimatum about whether or not they would stay at USC or transfer. The coach was shocked to hear that Bo and his friend decided to transfer to this school that didn't have a rich athletic tradition like USC. As per NCAA regulations, they sat out one year before they played in their first season for their new team. This basketball coach decided to play a "fast break" style, pushing the tempo of the game so that shots were attempted within a few seconds of their possession of the ball. On defense, they operated a full court press to force the other team into making turnovers. The strategy worked and played to the strength of the two transfer players.

Hank Gathers became a star on the Loyola Marymount University men's basketball team. The team set records for scoring including a 122.4 point per game average in Hank's senior year, where he led the country in both points and rebounds. In their game against International University, LMU scored an amazing 181 points. This is a feat that is unheard of and unseen today in NCAA Division 1 college basketball.

Gathers was pegged in his senior year to be a sure lottery pick for the NBA draft. On December 9, 1989, LMU was playing UC Santa Barbara when the star collapsed for no apparent reason while on the free throw line. Doctors found that he had an abnormal heartbeat and so he was given a beta blocker. Three months later, Gathers collapsed again in a game against Portland State. This time, he was not breathing. By the time he arrived at a nearby LA hospital, he was dead. LMU got to the NCAA basketball tournament and made it to the Elite Eight without Gathers, losing to the eventual champion, the University of

Nevada, Las Vegas. My daughter attended Loyola Marymount University some 15 years after the death of Hank Gathers and after classes she worked in the gym where Hank played. It is unofficially known as "Hank's House." His retired number hangs in the rafters, and the entire 1989-90 team was inducted into LMU's Sports Hall of Fame.

*

Dr. Mader made his concluding remarks, and it was now time for Dr. Prolis to speak on the topic. "Adoption of clinical practices, however appealing, requires evidence that such a strategy improves medical outcomes. There have not been any randomized trials conducted to show that exercise restriction of at-risk individuals decreases the incidence of sudden death. We don't even know what the incidence of sudden death is in the non-athlete. Nobody disputes the notion that regular exercise is beneficial to the heart. It may also be healthy in individuals who have a genetic myocardial defect. The studies conducted in Italy may not be applicable to our population. Italy has a special institute with doctors highly trained to interpret an ECG. They are solely responsible for their conclusions. In the U.S., these studies are conducted by specialists. We would have to set up an institute to duplicate their experience." Dr. Prolis had to counter Dr. Mader's highly emotional case with one of his own that was very different. "I had a patient who was a hockey player ..."

*

Bobby Carlsson and his family immigrated from Sweden where his father was a promising junior hockey player, but never good enough to play professionally. He and his wife moved to Minnesota when Bobby was 3 years old. Naturally, Bobby also took an interest in hockey. He was a strong skater and had a powerful slap shot. His coach put him on the right wing. When Bobby was 16, he was invited to join a team in the North American Hockey League, a tier II junior hockey program. Prior to joining the team, Bobby was required to undergo a physical examination including an electrocardiogram. He exhibited a right bundle-branch block in one of his lateral leads. Based on this preliminary finding, an echocardiogram was ordered which revealed a borderline ventricular enlargement. Bobby and his parents sat down with the cardiologist.

"What does this all mean?" his father asked.

"It might mean that you have hypertrophic cardiomyopathy. If you play a competitive sport like hockey, you may be at risk for a cardiac event."

"I feel fine doctor. There is nothing that will happen to me. Can you sign the paperwork so I can join the team?" Bobby was very anxious

"It is not that simple son," the doctor said. "You may be at risk for a sudden cardiac death."

Bobby's mom started to cry. "Are there some medications he may take so he can play safely?" Bobby's father asked.

"Yea, I'll take anything. Hockey means the world to me. I cannot give it up."

"I am recommending to the team that you see one of their cardiology specialists. I am sure there is something that can be done. Bobby and his parents left the doctor's office. Later, the team's specialist conducted more tests including putting Bobby on an exercise treadmill. When all of the tests were completed, Bobby and his parents were told that he had a mild form of hypertrophic cardiomyopathy. Playing hockey could risk his life. His junior hockey team revoked their invitation to play with them. Bobby was devastated. He became an angry teenager. He was mad at the world. He slowly drifted away from his friends. He left home after high school and got a job in construction. When Bobby was in his mid-twenties, he met a girl at work and soon they became close friends. She encouraged him to take up speed skating. There was one local club where all of the racers trained. It was not an expensive sport like hockey. Bobby had never really considered it before. He joined a local racing club and soon he was entering races. He threw cardiac caution to the wind and trained hard. Within a few years, Bobby became a district champion in the men's 5000 meters and qualified for the Olympic trials. Although Bobby never made it to the Olympics, he never suffered from any ill effects from speed skating.

*

With permission from the family, Dr. Prolis recounted Bobby's story and posed a hypothetical question to the audience. "Could he have been a professional hockey player? We never gave him the chance. In retrospect, it is likely that Bobby would have been fine in the junior hockey program. We may have caused him more harm by labeling him as a cardiac cripple. Fortunately for him, he was able to get past it, but how many others have we unnecessarily burdened?"

The question and answer section of the debate followed. Dr. Link was the moderator of the session. He congratulated both speakers for their excellent presentations and asked them to field questions from the doctors and scientists in the audience.

Sitting in the lecture hall and thinking about this debate, I wondered if any blood tests could be used for screening asymptomatic patients for the presence of hypertrophic cardiomyopathy. We have tests such as B-type natriuretic peptide that are important for heart failure and risk stratification for future adverse cardiac events. But blood levels are within the normal range in these subjects, so this is not an effective biomarker. I got up and asked one of the first questions.

"Are there protein or genetic markers available for screening hypertrophic cardiomyopathy?"

Dr. Mader responded. "There is active research going on in this area to discover new lab tests. There was a study conducted in Denmark and in other countries throughout the world and the data looks promising."

*

Dr. Jan Østergaard, a cardiologist and research scientist at Aarhus University Hospital in Denmark, received a call from a colleague in Sweden. Dr. Anhous was a noted expert in hypertropic cardiomyopathy. "I am following a family whose oldest son died of cardiomyopathy while playing soccer in school. Two years later, tragedy struck again to this family, as a second son collapsed and died on the basketball court. Thinking that there must be a genetic link, Dr. Mader suggested to the family that the remaining three children greatly restrict their physical activity. But then another child who was just walking to school on a cold day also collapsed and had to be resuscitated. Fortunately, she survived. I have told the family about your work in this field and they want to help. Can you see them?"

Dr. Østergaard was thrilled to get the call. *This may be the break we need*, he thought. It had been difficult for his research group to find a family of subjects who had this problem and were willing to participate. But the scientist had to be careful to not be overly jubilant considering the demise of several family members. "Can you set up an appointment for me to meet them and explain what is involved?"

Within a few weeks, the entire surviving members of the family flew to Aarhus University, funded by Dr. Østergaard's grants. It was important to fully characterize the family's cardiac status. After carefully explaining all of the steps to be taken, and the potential risks for each procedure, each member signed a consent form for participation in the research. Over the next several days, the adults and children underwent extensive invasive and non-invasive testing including electrocardiography, echocardiography, cardiac magnetic resonance imaging, CT angiography, cardiac catheterization, nuclear imaging, and even a cardiac biopsy. "Each of these tools gives us a different angle to the problem" he explained to the family and his staff. We need to know which of these tools will help us the most in predicting outcomes." He was careful to not state the outcome of "sudden death." Dr. Østergaard's staff collected four tubes of blood from each individual whom were to be used for an analysis of proteins and nucleic acids. "We need to know if there is a gene or protein that is causing this disease" he said.

*

Dr. Mader continued with his answer to my question. "After years of investigation in an affected family, Dr. Østergaard and his team identified a genetic mutation in a gene that encodes a protein called calmodulin. They are now trying to determine the incidence of this mutation in other individuals who have died of sudden cardiac death among athletes."

Dr. Prolis then responded. "Dr. Mader, recognizing that this mutation only explains one form of dilated cardiomyopathy, you will agree with me that this genetic test is not ready for routine use among athletes?"

"Clearly an economic analysis must be conducted to determine how much it would cost to conduct any laboratory screening tests and implement preventative measures with regard to the number of human lives saved. These studies have not been conducted. We do have to be careful not to make national healthcare decisions based the death of a few athletes."

*

It has been estimated that sudden cardiac death (SCD) claims the lives of over 300,000 Americans each year. The majority of these cases occurs in adults and is due to pre-existing diseases and conditions such as coronary artery disease, diabetes, hypertension, and smoking. Sudden death occurs because there is a disturbance in the electrical signals to the heart causing irregularities in the rhythms of the heart. In recent years, the implementation of implantable cardioverter defibrillators or ICDs has greatly reduced the rate of sudden cardiac death. These are mechanical devices that are inserted into the chest or abdomen of patients who are at high risk for SCD, i.e., patients who have survived a heart attack, have a history of abnormal heart rhythms, or have hypertrophic cardiomyopathy. ICDs monitor the heart rhythm and automatically deliver an electrical shock when it detects a fast and abnormal cardiac rhythm. Mutations in over 400 genes have been identified as being linked to inherited forms of SCD. Testing is available through specialized commercial reference laboratories.

Hypertropic cardiomyopathy accounts for only a minority of the cases of SCD. Besides the electrocardiogram, there are no routine genetic tests or protein markers that are available for athletes. The debate regarding the efficacy of ECG screening continues. The National Heart, Lung, and Blood Institute formulated a working group to identify and address gaps in the scientific and medical knowledge. A registry of cases is needed to determine the epidemiology of the disease. Controlled research trials must be conducted to evaluate the performance of pilot ECG screening programs, develop therapeutic strategies for asymptomatic subjects deemed to be at high risk and evaluate the economic impact. Until such screening programs are proven to be effective, it is up to each sports program and the individual family members to determine if they should undergo testing to make decisions regarding athletic participation.

Billy Jean-etics

"Raise your right hand." The woman complied. "Do you swear to tell the whole truth and nothing but the truth?"

"I will," she said.

"Please tell the court your name, and spell your last name."

"Debra Murray. M-U-R-R-A-Y."

You may be seated.

The district attorney, Mr. Frank DeMarco began his examination. "Can you tell us what you do for a living?"

"I am a visiting nurse," Debra replied.

"Who is your employer?" The DA asked.

"Dr. Robert Conrad," the witness replied.

"Is Dr. Conrad the defendant in this case?" Mr. DeMarco asked.

"Yes. He is seated over there with his defense counsel."

*

Two years earlier, Dr. Robert Conrad was a member of a group medical practice. Their firm was known as the "Doctors to the Stars." They had a reputation of being highly qualified, always available at any hour of the day, and willing to travel to all parts of the world at a moment's notice. Most important of all, the medical information on their clients was kept private and completely away from the public eye. All of the physicians had admitting privileges to Los Angeles' Cedar Sinai whenever hospitalization was necessary. One day, the head of the practice, Dr. Seymour Marmour called Dr. Conrad, a junior member of the practice, into his office. Dr. Conrad was 5 years removed from his UCLA residency program in internal medicine where he was the chief resident.

"What's up Sy?" Dr. Conrad asked.

"One of our clients is going on a world concert tour and wants a full time physician as part of the entourage," Dr. Marmour said.

"Does the client have continuing medical issues that warrant a full time doctor on staff?" Dr. Conrad asked.

"No, he has insomnia and wants someone who can prescribe strong medications for sleep," replied Conrad's boss.

"This doesn't seem a good use of my time. Why can't he hire a nurse?"

"He has a traveling nurse, but she is not authorized to prescribe DEA's list of Scheduled Drugs." Dr. Conrad knew that many of the sleep aids and anti-anxiety drugs were on the Department of Drug Enforcement's list of controlled substances. These drugs have therapeutic and abuse potential and are therefore put on "Schedules," a list of drugs that require dispensing only by highly qualified physicians. "He has a prescription for zolpidem and Xanax but he wants to get something more powerful," Dr. Marmour told his subordinate. "The singer is willing to pay $150,000 a month."

"Who are we talking about?" Dr. Conrad wanted to

know.

"It's Michael Jackman. Think it over Rob."

*

In the pop music world, there were few entertainers more popular and revered than Michael Jackman. He started his career as a child in a group that consisted of his older brothers, known as the Jackman 6. In addition to a crisp voice, Michael had a stage presence that world had not seen before. His dance moves were fluid and captivating. Over the next 40 years, Michael produced several of Billboard Magazine's top songs and albums, award winning music videos, television specials, full-length movies, and world concert tours. His sisters also became widely successful solo artists.

Now nearing 50 years old, Michael was slowing down. While he still loved to perform on stage, it was the day-to-day grind of traveling from city to city that took its toll on Michael's body and psyche. Michael would take long baths each night after a performance to ease muscle pain. He took a variety of analgesics including Percocet, Dilaudid, and Vicodin to dissociate his mind from these aches. His inability to sleep at night was the biggest health issue. His doctors gave him the sleeping aid, zolpidem, which was initially effective. However, when that drug alone stopped working, they added an anti-anxiety medications such a lorazepam and valium. Soon he was on a cocktail of several drugs. Few people outside the entertainment world can understand the strain of performing at a rock concert for several hours, especially for those who do both singing and dancing. The excitement of performing in front of tens of thousands of fans invokes an immediate and sustained adrenaline rush. The volume of the music and the flashing of strobe lights at unnatural frequencies exacerbate the situation for some individuals. High body and room temperatures further fatigues the performer. Immediately after the show, Jackman would experience exhaustion due to the prolonged mental stimulation. This is to the extent that sleep is impaired. The next day, the already tired musician had another show, and so the cycle would repeat.

*

Dr. Conrad felt hesitant to accept this assignment. He went home and discussed the offer with his wife. Cloris was very attractive and was seven years younger than Robert. They met at a diner near the UCLA Medical School campus where she was a waitress. Robert would go there frequently for a late evening dinner after his shift in the hospital ward. He was attracted to Cloris and usually sat at one of her tables. Robert was a plain looking man who could never get the pretty girls in school. But Cloris wanted to be a doctor's wife so she welcomed his company. Soon they began dating and by the time he finished residency, they were married.

"Are you kidding me Robert? Think of what this will do for your career. He is the King of Pop. With this work on your resume, you will be in demand. You can open up your own medical practice and not have to share your stipend with the partners. They don't deserve your dedication. Just think, $150,000 per month is close to $2 million per year. And that's just the start." Cloris was clearly seeing the dollar signs. "We could move to Beverly Hills, join a country club and finally have the life we deserve. I mean, what could possibly go wrong?"

Cloris was also thinking that it might be time to get

210

breast implants. The following Monday, he told Dr. Marmour that he would take the assignment and a meeting was arranged between them and the singer and Hector, his agent.

"I need someone who will do whatever it takes to keep me healthy to perform. The medications I have been given are too weak. Can you prescribe stronger drugs?"

"We have some anesthetics that will allow you to get the rest you need." Dr. Conrad was briefed as to the cause of his medical problems. "They are short acting, so you will be ready to go the next morning."

"Now you're talking doc. When can you start? We leave for the tour in three weeks."

Michael Jackman left the contractual details with Hector. They arranged for Dr. Conrad and Cloris to move into an apartment within Michael's mansion so that the patient could get better acquainted with the doctor before leaving for the concert tour. Dr. Conrad assembled his medical supplies and their personal effects and arrived at the Jackman estate a few days later. Hector was there to meet them at the door and gave the pair a tour of the property.

"So this is how the rich and famous live," Cloris said.

"Settle down, Cloris. This is my place of employment," Robert said to his wife.

"Does he have a spa here?" Cloris asked the agent.

"Naturally" Hector said. "We have a sauna, Jacuzzi baths, hot tub, massage room, exercise room, basketball court, bowling alley, tennis court, dance studio, music room, a movie theater with 50 seats, three swimming pools, everything Michael might ever need."

"This is so cool!" Cloris was awed by the celebrity's status. "When can I meet him?"

Michael was in the next room. Cloris was wearing a body clinging blouse, a short skirt, and pretty gladiator sandals. The singer heard her voice and came into the room. "So you are Cloris? I have heard a lot about you. I hope we can become friends."

"I am a big fan of yours Mr. Jackman. I have all of your albums."

Robert Conrad was uncomfortable with this dialog. "Can I see your medical facilities?" he asked.

"Of course, Dr. Conrad. Hector, can you show the good doctor what we have here? He can tell us what equipment we will need while we're on the road."

*

Robert Conrad made sure that Cloris was not part of the traveling entourage. Her presence would have been a distraction to both him and Michael too. After the first few shows, there would be many women would come to his hotel suite where they would smoke dope and Michael would take pain killers. As part of the contract, Hector agreed that Michael would take no recreational drugs. When the party was over each night, Michael retired to his bedroom where Dr. Conrad would administer his sleep medications. At first, Michael's sleeping pattern was excellent. He typically went to bed around 2 am and awoke at 9 am with a solid 7 hours of sleep. Debra Murray was hired and stayed in the next room monitoring Michael's sleep. While he had sex with many women, they were not allowed to stay overnight in the singer's bed. Dr. Conrad also prohibited the use of erectile dysfunction drugs.

Toward the end of the tour, Michael was getting more fatigued with every city and each show. Just as he feared, the sleep medications he was given were becoming increasingly less effective. Michael began to plead with Dr. Conrad to give him something stronger. Dr. Conrad was prepared for this request. He previously told Hector that he would have anesthetics. Now it was time to use them. With Nurse Debra Murray's assistance, they established an intravenous line in Michael's left arm. He wore a white glove on stage on his right hand. Dr. Conrad didn't want to interfere with that stage image. Once IV access was established, Dr. Conrad slowly infused a low propofol dose. Within minutes, Michael Jackman was asleep. Due to the potential dangers of the drug, Dr. Murray and Debra took turns staying with Michael as he slept, and act should there be any sign of trouble.

Debra took the first shift. Michael was sleeping soundly with no evidence of laboring. Debra sat next to his bed reading People Magazine, where there was a story on Michael's world tour. At 4 am, Dr. Conrad awoke from his nap, went into the room and relieved Debra.

"He's sleeping like a log, Doctor," she said. "The propofol is working well."

"Very good. I'll see you in the morning," Dr. Conrad said.

For the next two hours, Michael Jackman continued to be resting. Dr. Conrad got up to go to the bathroom and get another cup of coffee. While he was out of the room, Michael's breathing began to labor. The color in his face began to change from red to ashen. The singer was dying. When Dr. Conrad returned, he saw the dramatic change in his patient. But he did not have a crash cart, any resuscitation equipment, or an oxygen tank. He shook Michael's body in hopes reviving him. He called out to Debra to assist him. Together, they initiated mouth-to-mouth CPR including chest compressions. But it was to no avail. The two of them could not bring him back to consciousness, and Michael Jackman died.

*

"Ms. Murray, were you in the decedent's bedroom when he first began to have difficulty in breathing?" the prosecuting attorney Demarco asked.

"No, I was on break. Dr. Conrad was on duty at the time."

"Do you know how many minutes elapsed before he alerted you to assist?"

"I was asleep, but I think it was about 10 to 15 minutes."

"Did you have any emergency equipment available to you during the resuscitation attempt?"

"No, this was a hotel room, not a hospital."

"No basic or advanced emergency airway equipment?"

"No."

"No suction apparatus, or IV infusion pump?"

"No."

"No alarmed pulse oximeter?"

"No."

"No continuous monitoring equipment?"

"No."

"How much time elapsed before you called 911?"

"About 30 minutes."

"Why did you wait so long?

"We thought we could revive him."

After about another hour of this rigorous examination, DA Demarco finally said, "I have no further questions of this witness." The defense attorney, Mr. Harrison Rodel had no questions and Debra was excused. "We call Dr. Franklin Sato to the stand." Dr. Sato was the toxicologist at the medical examiner who analyzed Michael Jackman's postmortem fluids.

After some questions about Dr. Sato's education background, experience and employment history, DA Demarco went into the meat of his testimony. "What drugs did you find in the blood of Mr. Jackman?"

"We found a propofol concentration of 2.5 mg/L, lorazepam at 0.14 mg/L, 4.6 mg/L of midazolam, and a lidocaine of 0.7 mg/L," Dr. Sato said.

"Were any of these drugs found in toxic concentrations?" Demarco asked.

The propofol concentrations in the postmortem blood are within the range of values reported in other confirmed propofol-related deaths. I conclude that this drug, in conjunction with the others, was the manner by which Mr. Jackman died.

"Your witness," Demarco said.

"Dr. Sato, isn't it true that drugs redistribute from tissues to increase the concentrations seen in postmortem blood?" Demarco asked.

"Yes, but we conducted the autopsy within a few hours after death minimizing the postmortem redistribution phenomenon," Dr. Sao said.

"But there is no way to know for sure what the drug levels were at the time of death?" Rodel asked.

"It is likely that the levels were still lethal at the time of death."

"I move to strike that last statement as being speculative," Rodel said, requested a ruling.

"Overruled. The witness is a qualified expert" the judge ruled.

"I have no further questions of this witness," Rodel concluded.

"Judge, may we have a recess to consider the testimony we have heard today?" Rodel asked the judge.

"Agreed. Court is adjourned until tomorrow at 9 am," the judge said.

In private chambers, Harrison Rodel met with Dr. Conrad. "We're losing this case. You did not follow standard procedures when using this drug and your patient died. You are facing manslaughter charges and a prison sentence. I think we need to negotiate a plea bargain."

"No, there must be another way. I have used propofol many times and have never experienced any deaths. He must be genetically predisposed to having this problem. There must be something more we can do." Dr. Conrad was desperate.

"I know a colleague, Brenden Collins who was involved with a vehicular manslaughter case of a man who was intoxicated with codeine. They performed DNA analysis on the defendant and found that he was a slow drug metabolizer. There was a lab doctor from the General who performed the analysis and testified in court that the defendant was not impaired. Upon retrial, the driver was exonerated. Let me contact the doctor and see if he can help.

*

The national media covered the proceedings of the trial each day. I was not particularly interested in this case so I was not following the details. It came as a surprise when I got a call from Brenden Collins.

"Doc, you helped us with Nick Newman case a few years back. Do you remember it?" Collins asked.

"Sure, he was a poor metabolizer for cytochrome 2D6."

"Right. Well, we need your help again. Have you been following the Conrad case?"

"I tried not to but it has been everywhere. Why do you ask?"

"Dr. Conrad does not think he overdosed Michael Jackman with propofol and believes that the singer had some genetic predisposition towards the drug's toxic effects. Is this something you can help us with?" Collins said. "By the way, we expect the prosecution to rest in the next few days so we will need to mount a defense real fast."

I am no expert in propofol metabolism so I spent the next day examining the literature. Then I found plan the defense could use, so I met with attorneys Collins and Rodel after court.

"Propofol is principally metabolized by three enzymes. Cytochrome 2B6, 2C19, and UGT1A9. The first enzyme converts the drug to a hydroxyl form. The second adds a sugar molecule to the structure. There is a some prevalence of the variances in these enzymes among African Americans. They have a reduced capacity to break down propofol in order for it to be cleared naturally by the body. If we can get permission from the court to get DNA from the decedent, we can see if he is a slow metabolizer. Is the medical examiner and Mr. Jackman's family cooperative?"

"Actually, they are both very helpful," Rodel said. "They only want to know the truth of what happen. It is the District Attorney and the State of California that is out for a pound of flesh. I think we can get the court's permission to obtain DNA for your analysis. But they probably won't issue a continuance, so we have to act fast."

Samples were received in my laboratory and we performed sequencing of the 2B6, 2C19, and UGT genes using "next generation" technology. When the work was completed, I was brought to testify on behalf of the defense.

After the usual qualification questions, Rodel posed the principal question. "Doctor, what did you find in Mr. Jackman's blood?"

"There was a G516T mutation in CYP2B6 and C1399T mutation in UGT1A9. As these enzymes are needed to break down propofol, I characterize the decedent as a poor metabolizer," I responded.

"And what does that mean in this case?" Rodel asked.

"While a typical dose for someone who doesn't carry this mutation is safe, in my opinion, Mr. Jackman genetic makeup was such that this same dose toxic for him."

"Is genotyping typically performed for patients on propofol?" Rodel asked.

"No, routine tests for these genetic variances are not widely available, only under research settings. Dr. Conrad followed approved dosing procedures."

After a few more days of testimony by other experts, the defense rested. The prosecution argued that the doctor was negligent in not having standard emergency equipment available. The jury found him innocent of the original charge of involuntary manslaughter, but he was convicted of negligence. His medical license was revoked for 2 two years and he was placed on probation without prison time.

*

Propofol is primarily used for induction and maintenance of short-term anesthesia prior to surgery and for critical care patients on a ventilator. It is not approved as a sleep aid. Unlike recreational drugs and pain medications, propofol is not available on the street, and therefore it is not an abused drug by the general public. The drug has a short half-life of a few hours. Studies have shown that individuals with 2B6, 2C19, and UGT1A9 mutations have higher peak drug levels, but results are far from being definitive, making it difficult to conclude cause of death in any single case.

Michael Jackson died on June 25, 2009 and is remains are interred at the Forest Lawn Cemetery in Los Angeles. Dr. Conrad Murray was charged with involuntary manslaughter. The jury found Murray negligent for giving propofol along with sedatives including lorazepam. He also did not have the necessary life support and resuscitation equipment in case of an emergency. He should not have used a dangerous drug outside of a medical environment. In addition, he used propofol "off label," that is, not within the FDA-approved medical indications. While this practice is common for other drugs, this is not the case for propofol due to its dangerous profile. Dr. Murray was given a 4-year sentence, and was released after two due to prison overcrowding and good behavior. There was no pharmacogenomics tests conducted on the King of Pop. Jackson was not naïve to propofol as depicted in this story. An anesthesiologist had administered this drug for sleep while he was on tour in Europe a few years before his death. Therefore, it is unlikely that he was not genetically predisposed to the drug's toxicity.

Pharmacogenomics testing is not routinely used today by forensic pathologists to interpret postmortem drug levels for cases where there is an overdose of prescription drugs. It is possible that more testing of this type will occur for the investigation of post mortem drug overdoses, especially in high profile cases such as the Jackson case.

Revenge

There was a buzz in the office. Everyone in the break room heard the news.

"The creep is getting out on probation," one lab tech said.

"I can't believe he only served 7 years. What is wrong with our justice system?" said another.

Calvin was in his office and didn't hear the news. Nobody went in to ask him about it. Calvin never spoke to anybody in the office about Jaco or the death of his wife and daughter. In the last 7 years, he was totally immersed in his company. The company Test-Me, Inc. grew to nearly 50 employees and was a multimillion dollar enterprise. A major part of his company was marketing. They used all kinds of strategies to sell their adulteration products, herbal medications and hormones. This included ads within social media, attending conventions, having booths at sporting events, placing ads in fitness magazines. Secretly, Calvin's group had regular communications with the agents of important pros in nearly all sports. Calvin did not have time for dating or contemplating a second family. His only outlet was working out in the gym and drinking with some of his gym rat friends.

Eventually, Calvin received a text from his attorney. Jaco was granted parole on his sentence and was released from prison. When Jaco was originally sentenced, Calvin waived his right to be notified of his parole hearing. At that time, he didn't want anything to do with Jaco. But now, years later, Calvin stared at his smart phone for several minutes upon learning that the murderer of his family was getting out. There wasn't a week that went by that he didn't think about his wife and his daughter Jenny. She would be a teenager right now. She would have been a great student. She would be thinking about boys right about now.

I can't let this happen, he thought to himself. *He may have paid his debt to society, but he hasn't paid his debt to me. I will not forgive him. This is not the end of this story.*

For the next several months, Calvin investigated on how to kill someone without getting caught. He got a wig and dark glasses to disguise himself. He went to the public library to search on the internet for information about poisons. He knew a lot already about this subject.

*

When Jaco first entered prison to serve his sentence, doctors saw that he was heavily addicted to opiates. He underwent a rigorous rehabilitation program with methadone and later buprenorphine. These drugs are used to slowly wean individuals off of heroin or morphine, while minimizing the withdrawal symptoms. At first, the inmates abused him verbally and sexually for being responsible for the death of a child. Eventually when his fellow prisoners and guards saw that he was harmless, he was accepted. From that point on, he was a model prisoner. He worked on construction hoping to land a job once he made parole. When we received his release, Jaco's parole officer arranged a job for him working in construction. He was the "shovel man," the guy who distributes concrete poured out of a truck and onto a mold used to make a city sidewalk. It was hard work but he was happy to be out of the joint.

*

Calvin was thinking that if he wanted to kill Jaco for what he did to his family, how would he do it and escape attention. He didn't think he had the nerve to shoot, stab, or blow up the culprit. He needed something more subtle. He had access to a variety of drugs, chemicals and poisons and felt this would be more his style. Calvin went online to read about deaths caused by unusual poisonings and how the murderer was caught. He found many cases about hospital workers killing their patients. He first read about Kristen Gilbert, the nurse who was convicted of murdering several Veterans Administration patients by injecting them with overdoses of epinephrine. She may have reasoned that many of her victims were elderly and were going to die anyway. Then there was Ann Miller Kontz who pled guilty to murder and conspiracy to kill her husband Eric Miller by arsenic poisoning. Her boyfriend committed suicide shortly after Miller's death although in his suicide note, he denied any involvement with the murder. Anesthesiologist, Dr. Carl Coppolino, injected the anesthetic succinylcholine to kill his wife, mistress, and the mistress' husband in 1966 and 1967. Calvin learned that this poison is nearly impossible to detect in postmortem tissue because the drug metabolizes quickly to choline and succinic acid, both natural ingredients found in the body. Christina Marie Riggs was executed in Arkansas for the murder of her two young children while they slept. She attempted to kill them with an injection of potassium chloride. When it was unsuccessful, she smothered them each with a pillow. In a twist of irony, Riggs was found guilty of first degree murder and was executed with a lethal injection of potassium chloride.

I have many of these chemicals and drugs in my lab and could easily use them on Jaco given the opportunity, Calvin thought. *But unless he is in some medical facility, it would be hard to intravenously inject him with anything through a syringe like some of these other murderers did. But maybe there is a better way....*

*

Given that Jaco's crime involved the abuse of heroin, the terms of Jaco's parole included strict abstinence from any drug or alcohol use. He was subject to regular drug testing and inspection of his living quarters. Jaco's parole officer made it clear that any violation would result in parole revocation and an immediate return to prison to resume his sentence. Jaco was happy to be out and willingly abided by these stipulations. His prison experience made Jaco a new man. He turned to religion and regularly attended the prison's church services. He read the Bible every night while he was alone in his cell. Jaco was never an evil man, just one who got caught up in drug addiction as a young adult.

One of the first things Jaco did when released was to join a local church, who took him without any reservations or questions about his past. Jaco attended sermons every Sunday and volunteered his time at night, doing odd jobs for the pastor. He did not go to any bars or night-clubs after work and was not tempted by drugs or alcohol. That part of his life was a distant memory. Within a few months, Jaco started seeing a woman named Toni. As a child, Toni was abused by her uncle and had significant psychological issues with men. Jaco was gentle with her and soon they were inseparable.

*

Under an assumed name, Calvin hired a private investigator to find out where Jaco was living. The investigator was not told nor did he ask why Calvin wanted this information. When he got the address, Calvin paid the PI and told him that he no longer needed his services. Over the course of the next several weeks, Calvin traced Jaco's daily habits, including the hours he worked, the days that he was at church, and when he was home. After a pattern was established, Calvin was ready to attack. During a work day, Calvin broke into the basement of Jaco's apartment through an unlocked window. Calvin was in his disguise, but nobody noticed his entry. Jaco lived in a one-bedroom apartment in the basement. There was a closet where there was a small gas furnace. It was autumn and the furnace was not turned on yet for the winter season. As he suspected, the furnace was very old and poorly maintained. Calvin examined the filter and noticed that it was very dirty and clogged. The combustion chamber had some rusty pipes. Calvin took out an awl and with a hammer, poked some additional small holes into the pipes. He then went looking for the smoke and carbon monoxide detectors in the apartment. When he located them, he noticed that the detectors were not hardwired to the house. Therefore, the insertion of a dead battery would not trigger an alert. These detectors would signal an alarm when the battery was losing its power, but not when it was completely dead as there would be no power to signal the alert. Calvin flipped open the lid removed the 9-volt battery from each detector, replacing them with the dead one that he brought.

Calvin then inspected all of the windows of the apartment to make sure that they were sealed shut. *I don't want any more air circulation in this room than absolutely necessary.* Calvin left the apartment through the open window closing it shut from the outside. The former clinical laboratory scientist then walked around to the back of the apartment looking for the exhaust pipe to the furnace in Jaco's room. When he found it, he climbed up to the roof, gathered some leaves and sticks, and crammed the exhaust pipe to block the outflow of air. *This is going to get you one day soon. I hope you die slowly and in plenty of agony*, he thought as he was leaving the premise.

*

About a month later, Jaco and Toni went to Jaco's apartment after spending an hour at church. She had been unofficially living there. They ordered takeout from a Chinese restaurant and were having dinner together. After their meal, they sat on the couch to watch a show about the Alaskan wilderness.

"It's cold in here, can you turn on the heat?" Toni asked Jaco.

"I kind of like it cold. It forces us to snuggle more," Jaco said.

"No really, I am shivering. If you don't do it, I'm going to leave."

"Alright, I'll do it. Give me a second," Jaco responded.

Jaco got up and went to the kitchen to get some matches and a flashlight. He then went into the closet and opened the furnace hatch. He turned the gas valve to the on position and tried to light the pilot.

"The match keeps blowing out," Jaco said. "Couldn't we just use a space heater? I will call the apartment super in the morning?"

"I'm cold. Can you light it please?" was Toni's response. Those were the last words she would ever speak again.

After about 10 more minutes of trying and after using a full book of matches, Jaco succeeded in lighting the pilot. He then closed the hatch and walked over to the thermostat on the wall. The temperature was 61 degrees. *No wonder she's cold,* he thought. Jaco turned the thermostat to 70 degrees. Within a few moments, he heard the flame within the furnace kick in. Heat was coming out of the radiators.

"Happy now?" he asked her.

Ton nodded. *I'm smug as a bug* she thought to herself.

The pair went back to the couch to watch the rest of the show. While embracing Jaco, Toni fell asleep first. Then Jaco nodded off with the TV still on. The furnace was running strong. But there was a slow leak of an odorless and invisible gas slowly and quietly polluting the room air.

A few hours later, Jaco woke up with a terrible headache. He got up and staggered to the bathroom looking for some aspirin. He was dizzy and his vision was blurred. He found the bottle and took a couple of pills and went back to the sofa where Toni was sleeping. After 20 minutes, Jaco awoke again being very nauseous. His headache was worse. He shook Toni to see if she was feeling alright, but to his surprise, he could not arouse his girlfriend. Toni was unconscious. Jaco jumped up and rushed to the phone. He called 9-1-1 and told them they had an emergency. By the time the ambulance arrived a few minutes later, Jaco had collapsed onto the floor and was also unconscious. The paramedics knocked on the door. With no one to answer the knock, one of the paramedics broke the door down. They found the pair unconscious. They were quickly transported to the

General Hospital.

Jaco and Toni were put into separate adjacent rooms within the ED. Claire, the ER nurse, installed a pulse oximeter device onto the right index finger of both patients. Within a few seconds, she had a reading and was reporting the results to Dr. Mary Stuart who was the attending doctor.

"Doctor, the pulse ox is normal at 98% saturation." The degree by which arterial blood is oxygenated is measured by the device.

"This is likely an incorrect reading. We need to get a blood gas and co-oximeter panel sent" Dr. Stuart said. "The clinical laboratory test is more accurate for cases like these."

Claire did not know what the doctor meant by "cases like these." She was puzzled as to how the doctor knew that the pulse ox reading was wrong.

Under Dr. Stuart's supervision, a small sample of blood was removed from an artery in the neck of both patients and sent to my laboratory for blood gases and a co-oximetry panel. Normally, arterial blood is 95% to 99% saturated with oxygen. We reported the result within 5 minutes of receipt of the sample in the laboratory. The oxygen saturation in Jaco and Toni's blood was below 65%. Instead of oxygenated blood, Jaco and Toni's blood contained a 25% and 31% concentration of "carboxyhemoglobin."

"These patients have been exposed to carbon monoxide, probably from a gas leak in their home," Dr. Stuart said to Claire.

"We need to call the Department of Public Health who can send an investigator to verify the cause. Please contact the proper authorities," he said to Claire.

"I'll get right on it." *Dr. Stuart was right on this one,* Claire thought. *I guess all that training on the value and limitations of clinical lab tests has paid off for her.*

Word of the carbon monoxide poisoning spread through the lab. I took this opportunity to bring my medical technologists to the emergency department where we met Dr. Stuart who was at the nurse's station just outside Jaco's room. In hopes of replacing carbon monoxide with oxygen, both Jaco and Toni were put on a mask connected to a tank that contained pure oxygen.

"Human hemoglobin has a greater than 200-fold higher affinity for carbon monoxide than oxygen," Dr. Stuart told my students. "This means that our patient's tissues were being starved of the oxygen it needs to function."

"What else can we do to save these two?" one of my students asked.

"We are making arrangements to transport these patients to the naval base. They have a hyperbaric chamber that can pump pure oxygen at three times the normal atmospheric pressure." Dr. Stuart then went on to explain that these "dive" chambers were used to treat sailors who suffered from decompression sickness, also known as "the bends." Scuba divers who breathe through air tanks underwater under high pressure can have nitrogen gas leak into their blood and tissues if they attempt to rise too quickly from the deep. An ambulance was called to transfer Jaco and Toni to the base. Unfortunately, Toni died on route. Jaco made it to the hyperbaric chamber but it was also too late for him as well. Jaco's parole officer was notified about his death. Nobody could locate Toni's Uncle.

A few days later, Calvin read in the paper about the deaths of Jaco and Toni in a short article near the back of the "Metro" pages. Public health officials found a leaky furnace and poor ventilation as the cause. Their deaths were listed as "accidental" by the medical examiner, and no further investigations were conducted by law enforcement. A smirk ran across Calvin's face. While Calvin was sorry that an innocent woman also died, he thought that *Jaco got what he deserved.* It had been 8 years since the death of his wife and child. During this time, an evil man turned good and a good man turned evil.

*

Carbon monoxide poisoning is responsible for about 40,000 ED cases per year, resulting in about 5000 deaths per year. The majority of household exposures occur in the cold parts of the U.S. and are caused by faulty heaters and furnaces. In addition to impairing the delivery of oxygen to respiring tissues, carbon monoxide also binds to other important proteins such as myoglobin, cytochromes and NADPH reductase. These moieties are essential in the body's ability to produce energy. Cyanide is another gas that is highly toxic to human tissues. This poison is sometimes released in houses on fire, but unlike carbon monoxide, cyanide is not released following incomplete fuel combustion.

Early generation pulse-oximeters only measure oxygenated and reduced forms of hemoglobin. When carboxyhemoglobin is present, it is registered as the oxygenated form, and for carbon monoxide poisoned patients it gives doctors the wrong information. Recently, pulse oximeters are available that can measure carboxyhemoglobin and can be used for CO poisonings. However, this technology has not been widely implemented in ED labs, and the co-oximetry test from the clinical laboratory is the most accurate. Some patients have high concentrations of methemoglobin due to the exposure of drugs and chemicals such as amyl nitrite and other nitrite containing compounds. This chemical is available in small canisters called "poppers." Poppers are inhaled to enhance a sexual experience and are abused by young adults. Like carboxyhemoglobin, patients with this form of hemoglobin also have poor oxygenation of the tissues and pulse oximeters produce incorrect results.

I hesitated to write this story about a crime of this nature because accidental carbon monoxide poisoning is common for people who live in old homes. Newer homes and apartments have better protection against leaky furnaces. Houses heated by electricity do not have this problem at all.

Although Calvin felt some justice for avenging the death of his wife and daughter, it was short lived. Within a few weeks, he was a victim of a random traffic accident when he entered an intersection after stopping. He was hit by a truck that came across his lane, having run a red light. He was taken to the hospital where...

Epilogue

****

This book is a slight departure from my previous books that featured the importance of clinical laboratory tests in solving medical mysteries or creating bad outcomes or disease through faulty decisions or interpretations. The stories in this book parallel cases that have occurred to celebrities and other well-known individuals.

Urine drug testing was enacted in 1988 by President Ronald Reagan as a means to combat drug and substance abuse. Public service messages regarding the effect of abuse on health were insufficient to convince individuals to abstain. It was also hoped that many individuals would stop abusing drugs if their employment and source of income were removed with a positive drug test. Drug testing programs among Federal employees and in the private sector undoubtedly reduced drug abuse, at least for the drugs that are routinely tested, notably cocaine, methamphetamine, heroin and other opiates, and marijuana. Abuse of other drugs such as tranquilizers and other hallucinogens are not tested and their abuse escapes detection.

Unfortunately, new products have been developed and sold, such as the one created by Calvin, to enable a drug user to cheat the drug testing process. It is unclear how much these commercial adulterants are used. However, an employee who is addicted to drugs does exhibit specific behaviors and eventually will get caught by the drug testing system.

The motives and scope of drug testing for athletes are different than for the workplace. Here, the objective is to "level the playing field" so that no individual athlete gets an unnatural and unfair competitive advantage. There are significant financial rewards for individuals and their current or future families who are at the very top of their sport. While there are reports that use of performance enhancing drugs can have significant long-term health issues, many young athletes either ignore these warnings, or willingly accept the risks. Some athletes believe that they cannot achieve their athletic goals without assistance. Others may believe that PED use is prevalent and their abstinence may put them at a disadvantage. Whatever the reason, PEDs specific for a particular sport are used by professional and amateur athletes despite the implementation of drug testing programs. Many of these testing programs are inadequate, especially for naturally occurring hormones where it is difficult to separate high levels due to abuse from naturally elevated concentrations due to human biologic variation. It has also been true that some sports programs do not want a completely comprehensive testing program. Major league baseball ignored steroid use by its players until individual records were shattered by players to the point that PEDs could no longer be ignored. PED use did lead to a revival of the game's interest through the creation of superstars.

As described in my book, there are other "assassins" that unknowingly affect the lives and health of our athletes. In order to achieve at the highest levels, these men and women willingly

234

subject their bodies to excessive training methods or they are pushed by their coaches and agents to take PEDs. No harm comes to the vast majority of these participants. However, there are a few individuals who are genetically predisposed to dangers from the rigors of exercise. When that happens, it is truly tragic because unlike those who cheat, these athletes did nothing to deserve the fate they received. Fortunately, it is a relatively rare occurrence, and when it does happen, measures may be taken by sporting organizations to prevent others from suffering.

Other books by this author, available through:

Toxicology! Because What You Don't Know Can Kill You.
Collection of short stories containing real toxicology cases.

<u>Online Reviews:</u>

I loved this book because of the short stories (I am a busy mom of 2 kids under the age of 4, so anything short and sweet is awesome). They were fascinating and captivating and very thought provoking! I particularly loved that the stories made me outraged at some behavior and sympathetic at others. Things that I never imagined could happen were mortifying to read and that's what I found especially captivating about this book from cover to cover! If you want to have your eyes opened and mind blown, you're absolutely going to be hooked!

Dr. Wu is a combination of Sherlock Homes and Dr. Watson. This book is not only fun to read, but it is also educational. The author breaks it down so even a lay person such as myself can understand it. The short-story writing style makes it feel like a quick read and keeps you turning the pages to discover the twist at each unique ending.

The Hidden Assassin: When Clinical Lab Tests Go Awry
Collection of true short stories containing real clinical laboratory cases.

<u>Online Reviews:</u>

This book of true medical short stories is fascinating. It kept my interest one after another. I had no intention of reading them all in one day, when I started. But each one was suspenseful, short and to the point; many, many times with surprise endings. I believe in recommending it so enthusiastically that I have purchased two extras as loners for friends! Alan Wu definitely is among my top authors since this book.

Although this book is broken down into independent cases, once you start it you will probably read the entire book in one night. Some of the cases in the book were actually headlined in the news which made it even more interesting. It is written in such a way that it can be enjoyed by professional toxicologists and also anyone who is just interested in the subject.

Microbiology! Because What You Don't Know Will Kill You.
Collection of true short stories containing real clinical
microbiology cases.

Online Reviews

Another excellent book by Dr. Wu bridging the worlds of
laboratory science and the patients. Two worlds usually separated
by a wall. Most people are heavily exposed to medical science~
pharmaceuticals, big radiology machines, or small glucose meters~
but very few are familiar with the clinical laboratory and the
tremendous impact it can have in their lives. Dr. Wu's books
open up that world with stories of common, and sometimes not
so common, people.

Dr. Wu continues to enlighten us about the importance of
knowledge. It is critical we take the time to learn what is actually
happening behind the scenes. Whether it be a simple blood or
urine test, or possible exposure to harmful microorganisms, or
drugs, we need to be more aware of our environment and the
control we have over it. I think our health care providers expect
and want us to take more responsibility for our own health. By
being more cognizant we can increase our odds of living a longer
and a healthier life.

CPSIA information can be obtained
at www.ICGtesting.com
Printed in the USA
BVHW072117010119
536803BV00020B/570/P